A Good Girl

A Charlie McClung Mystery

By Mary Anne Edwards

Publisher: CreateSpace Independent Publishing Platform
ISBN-13: 978-1500123581
ISBN-10: 1500123587

Cover Design – Jasmin Woodworth

Cover Photography by -
Tree-lined street: By maigi (Own work) [CC-BY-SA-3.0-ee
(http://creativecommons.org/licenses/by-sa/3.0/ee/deed.en)], via Wikimedia Commons

St Pancras Old Church: Stephen McKay
CC-BY-SA-2.0 (http://creativecommons.org/licenses/by-sa/2.0)], via Wikimedia Commons

To my husband, Jeff, for always believing in me.

I want to give a special thank you to Gina, my forever best friend, for her unending friendship and superb medical knowledge. Also, thank you to Melissa for her pathology and forensic wisdom, to retired Chief Mike Edwards for his interviewing advice, to my Aunt Mary Valdez for her knowledge of Catholicism, and to my parents, Mingo & Peggy Gonzales for their prayers. A big thank you to my proofreaders, Rick Caruso, Jeff Edwards, Amanda Marie, and Lynet Mortensen. My deep gratitude to Gretchen Smith, Tabitha Jones, Shelley Giusti, Tina Whittle, and Marie Nicoll. I can't forget my Street Team. THANK YOU!

Also by Mary Anne Edwards

Brilliant Disguise

Chapter 1

Charlie was scrawled across the envelope taped over the doorbell. Charlie McClung's heart pounded. *This can't be good.* His family had been dying to meet Marian Selby and this was the big day, the big reveal. So, for his family not to be standing in the driveway with open arms could only mean something horrendous had happened. He yanked the folded paper from inside the envelope and read the note written by his mother.

Don't worry, Love, we're all okay. Come to the shop. A dead girl was found in an armoire delivered just now. Huggies, Ma.

"What's the matter, Charlie?" Marian asked, staring at his wrinkled brow.

He sighed, "Oh, nothing. There's a dead girl at *The Antique Shop.*"

Marian's eyes grew wide and her mouth fell open. "Did you just say there's a dead girl at *The Antique Shop*? Your family's shop?"

"Yep." Charlie nodded. "Let's go." He grabbed her hand and started toward his car.

She didn't move. "That's it? Dead girl, let's go as if a dead girl is no big thing?"

He tugged her hand. "I'll explain on the way."

Once in the car, speeding toward Main Street, he gave her all the details he could. "So you understand now I wasn't making light of a girl's death. I was relieved my family was okay."

Marian reached over and rubbed his shoulder. "Yeah, not exactly the welcome you expected. Sorry, I sounded so gruff." She saw his smile smooth out the worry lines on his forehead.

Charlie clasped her hand and kissed it. "I love you, Marian Francis Selby, you know that? I'll always give you all the facts, never keep any secrets. You can count on that." He kissed her hand again before releasing it.

She sighed, "Yep, I know." Pausing she added, "I love you, too." Three months ago, she couldn't have thought she would ever say those three sacred words to any man again. In her mind, they belonged to her husband, Lee, who died 11 years ago. But so many things had happened in such a short time. Her good friend and neighbor was murdered, and the same lunatic would have killed her, if not for Charlie. Then Lee appeared to her one night somewhere between a memory and a dream and released her to Charlie's love.

Now, she was about to meet Charlie's family the same way she had met him, over someone's dead body. Staring out the car window, she watched his old neighborhood fly by as he drove to *The Antique Shop*. She caught bits and pieces of his family's world: large Victorian homes with gorgeous flowerbeds, well-maintained yards, and sidewalks shaded by arching Southern Live Oaks. Closing her eyes, Marian imagined Charlie as a little boy walking to school with his older brother and two younger sisters. She smiled thinking that there had probably been a lot of teasing, chucking acorns, and races to school.

Feeling a sharp right turn, she opened her eyes. They were going down Main Street, which was just as lovely as his old neighborhood. A large crowd had gathered in front of one of the long-standing stores. *The Antique Shop* was printed neatly in gold on a black sign above its door with a strip of bright yellow crime tape blocking its entrance. Several police cars and an ambulance were parked in front.

Charlie parked his 1967 Plymouth Belvedere GTX next to one of the police cruisers. Marian noticed Charlie clipping his badge on his belt as he walked directly toward the center of the mayhem.

An older officer with his thumbs hooked in his pant loops stood erect when he saw the two of them approaching. He put up a flat palm signaling them to stop. "This is an active crime scene. Please step …" The officer's stern face transformed into a welcoming smile. "Charlie, you old dog. I heard you were comin' up for a visit." He extended his hand. "Good to see you."

Shaking the officer's hand, Charlie replied, "Yeah, good to be back, Mike. Say, what's going on here?" Charlie pointed his chin toward the door of his family's shop.

Mike smiled. "You must be Marian. The whole town's been waitin' to meet the one who finally snagged ol' Charlie boy." He shook her hand gently. "My name's Mike. Mike Purvis."

Marian blushed. "Um, yeah, my pleasure to meet you, Mike. I didn't know Charlie was so popular." She grinned at Charlie who stood scratching his head. "I can't wait to meet everyone too." She studied Mike's pleasant face, guessing he was probably five years older than Charlie. He was tall, lean, and his dirty blonde hair had a buzz cut. His Siamese cat blue eyes revealed a happy soul. "So, I'm guessing you've known him for a while?" She leaned her head against Charlie as she entwined her arm around his.

Chuckling, Mike answered, "Known him practically all of his life." Noticing Charlie's exasperation, he cleared his throat. "Well, we can go into all of that later. I'm sure you want to know the details of what's happened. Don't you?"

"Walk me through it, sergeant." Charlie ducked under the single piece of crime tape. He held it up, motioning for Marian to join them.

As they hurried toward the back of the store, Marian gasped at the sight of the exquisite antiques. This had to be the most beautiful and organized antique shop she'd ever seen. It was as if she were walking through a museum. Her attention was torn away from the lovely pieces when she heard Mike say, "She was strangled, and a red rosary was stuffed in her mouth."

A sick feeling washed over her as they entered the dimly lit storage room. Slowing her steps, Marian wondered if she really wanted to be this close to Charlie's work.

A slight pull caused Charlie to turn. He saw Marian's pale cheeks and cupped her face. Staring into her eyes he said, "You can stay here if you'd rather not tag along."

Her mouth twitched with his concern and she felt like crying. Marian kissed his cheek. "Thank you, but I want to know what you feel. I want to understand, be a part of you."

A smile played on his full lips. "Okay, but at any time, you can leave and I'll understand. Okay?"

She nodded.

Sergeant Purvis interrupted. "Is she coming with?"

"Yes. Yes, I am," Marian answered with determination.

Pursing his lips and nodding, Purvis handed them each a pair of latex gloves. "All right then, put these on."

Charlie snapped on the gloves and then helped Marian with hers. "When did you start using these?"

"Oh, a few months ago thanks to your doctor brother-in-law and your niece, Mary Grace. Said we're livin' in the 80s now. Just because we're a small town doesn't mean we're immune from the big city problems." Purvis rubbed his gloved hands together. "Yep. Things have changed a lot since my rookie days," he added and headed toward the back door.

Purvis opened the heavy door. Bright sunlight flooded the storage room, along with sounds of the small mob that had gathered to witness the police investigation.

A cheer went up when Charlie stepped outside. "There he is, Ma. It's Charlie."

Three officers held back the McClung clan gathered just beyond the crime scene. "Stand back. Don't go tramping on evidence. Back up! Stay behind the tape."

"Oh, glory be, there she is!" exclaimed a mature lady with flaming red hair. She leaned against the bright yellow tape, motioning for Marian to come over.

Charlie whispered in Marian's ear. "That's Ma and the family. We better go over before the officers have to handcuff her."

Marian hesitated. Looking into his eyes, she murmured, "But I thought you were going to let me be a part of this?" She nodded toward the armoire standing in the parking lot five feet from the door they had exited. "To understand your work?"

Charlie kissed her forehead. "Family first." He guided her around the armoire toward his family. They went under the tape and into his mother's wide open arms.

Marian felt as if she would be crushed by all the arms that surrounded her. She looked for Charlie and saw him standing behind his mother. He laughed, mouthing, "They love you."

"All right now. Move back so I can get a good look at her." The crowd parted at Ma's command. "Ah, look at ya now. You're a pretty young thing. Isn't she, Da?"

An older version of Charlie appeared next to Ma. "Aye, she's a fine lookin' lass, that she is," Da answered as he stood with his arms crossed, looking her up and down.

Their lilting Irish accents made Marian smile.

Charlie wrapped his arm around Marian. "This is my mother, Mary Kathleen, and my father, John Patrick. Ma, Da, Marian."

The family as a whole embraced her, again. Each one introduced themselves to her, welcoming her into their clan. Marian was overwhelmed with their outpouring of love. Immediately, she felt like a part of them, as if she was their long-lost daughter.

"Hey! We've got a murder over here, Detective McClung. I could use your help," snarled a tall man in a dark business suit leaning against the armoire with his arms and ankles crossed.

Charlie smiled when he saw his baby sister's husband. Rachel had followed in Ma's footsteps and married a copper - an Irish one at that, Luke O'Sullivan. He clasped his brother-in-law's hand. "How are you doing, Luke? I heard you made detective."

Luke shrugged and motioned for him to follow. "I was doing okay until Rach called me all in a tizzy." He stopped just before rounding the armoire. Scratching his narrow chin he cocked his head toward Charlie. "Gotta be honest with you; this is my first homicide. Things like this don't happen in Mercy City, you know."

Charlie saw Luke swallow the nervous lump caught in his throat. "So what do you have?" When they rounded the antique armoire, he shook his head grimacing at the macabre sight of a young girl's body. She looked familiar. "Who is she?" he asked as he squatted to get a better look. She was tiny, about 5 feet tall and maybe 100 pounds. Her black hair was tangled in a slender red cord wound tightly around her swan-like neck. The cord was nothing extraordinary, red with tassels on each end. Cranberry red rosary beads were dangling from her bluish lips. Her thickly lashed brown eyes would have been beautiful if not clouded and frozen open in death.

"She's Jason and Becky Rogers' girl, Darla Jean. They reported her missing early this morning." Luke rubbed his face with both hands. "That's what makes it even tougher. I know them. My boy, Jack, went to school with her. Criminy, how am I going tell them their only child is dead?"

Charlie clasped Luke's shoulder. "I'll go with you. I know it'll be rough, and I can tell you from experience to expect anything from stunned silence to an all-out fight."

Luke patted Charlie's back. "Thanks."

Charlie glanced beyond the armoire. Marian, still wearing the latex gloves, appeared to be at ease with his exuberant family. He turned his attention to Luke, "Where's the M.E.?"

"Ah, Dylan's come and gone. Said he had a surgery and would see me at the funeral home and to bring ya along."

Charlie imagined his older sister's husband, Dr. Dylan Leech, rushing to the scene like that M.E. from the show *Quincy*. Dylan would say, "Yes, she is dead. Died from strangulation. Been dead for approximately 15 hours give or take. Gotta go. Surgery in an hour." Charlie cocked an eyebrow thinking Dylan kind of resembled the guy, as well.

Charlie glanced at the dead girl, then at Luke, and then toward the McClung clan. From death to life, and to a new beginning. "Well, Luke, want to say hello to Marian before we go inform the Rogers?"

"Yeah, she's all the McClung women have been talking about for months." Luke instructed the officers to fingerprint the armoire, top to bottom, inside and out. And to bag everything even if they didn't think it mattered, and to photograph everything before it was bagged. He gave the okay for Darla Jean to be taken to the morgue after she was photographed from all angles. After he was satisfied his commands were understood, Luke walked with Charlie to meet Marian.

Charlie's mother circled her arms around his waist, resting her head on the curve of his neck. "Ah, Charlie, my son, she's absolutely stunnin', I tell ya. Simply brilliant, she is."

He winked at Marian standing in between Rachel, his baby sister, and his Aunt Ella, who was wearing a pale lavender riding hat. She always wore a hat, no matter the occasion. Charlie pulled Marian next to him, sliding one arm around her waist and his other around Ma's. Kissing them both on their foreheads, he said, "My two favorite women in the world. How lucky am I?"

Da pulled his wife from Charlie. "Sorry, son, she's mine. Besides, ya got more than ya need with this lass." Charlie's father patted Marian's blushing cheek. "Ella," Da shouted at his sister. "Call it a day. Ya can't get anything done with the lot of them crawlin' around." He pointed toward the police bagging bits and pieces of possible evidence and snapping pictures. "Let's go home and get to know our Marian."

Luke extended his hand toward Marian. "Nice to finally get to meet you, Marian. I'm Luke."

"It's a pleasure meeting you."

Marian smiled as Rachel whispered in her ear, "This here copper is my husband. Isn't he lovely?"

Charlie tugged his ear, "Da, I can't go with you just now. Luke and I have a job to do. But take Marian." He squeezed Marian, "That's if you don't mind."

"No, go, I understand. I'd love to go with your family," Marian grinned.

Luke stepped back. He knew his father-in-law would not like Charlie's response. Family always came first and since Charlie moved away from Virginia, he didn't work for Mercy City. And he was on vacation to be with family, not to help solve a murder. So, Luke was surprised when Da smiled.

Da patted Charlie's back. "I understand, son, it's in ya blood." He peered at Luke, then leaned toward Charlie and winked, "The boy's gonna need ya son. Still wet behind the ears, he is." Then Da said in a loud voice as he squeezed Marian's hand, "We can educate your lass. She'll get the unedited version of ya life."

Charlie instructed Marian, "Now, don't you believe a word." He pointed at Da. "And you, don't scare her away with your fancy lies. I don't want to lose her."

Ma shushed her husband. "Keep ya voices down." Her eyes cut toward the armoire. "Have ya no respect for the dead?"

The McClung clan hushed. Aunt Ella's hands trembled as she dabbed her eyes and red nose with a dainty lavender handkerchief. She was the one who had opened the armoire.

Marian saw Charlie's jaw tighten when he looked at the crime scene. "Charlie, can I see?"

He nodded, then clasped her hand with Luke leading the way. Charlie paused behind the armoire, "Are you sure you want to do this?"

She murmured, "Yes, I need to do this. If your family can, I can too."

He knew she was right. It was the family's shop, so the family was involved and Marian was family.

Luke lifted the yellow tape and she ducked under.

"Oh, Charlie, she's just a baby." Tears filled her eyes. She'd seen death, but only in movies. A familiar ache clutched at her as she thought of the girl's family. Were they waiting for their little girl to come bouncing through the front door, asking what was for dinner? Or were they already grieving? She scanned the girl's body stopping at her huge brown eyes. What did they see before she died? The claw marks on the girl's pale neck were evidence of the futile attempt she'd made to save her life.

A tissue appeared before Marian. She took it, giving Charlie a strained smile. "I've seen enough," she mumbled into Charlie's broad chest as he encircled her with his arms and kissed the top of her head. "Are you okay?"

Marian wiped her nose and nodded. "You and Luke have to find whoever did this."

"Are you sure you're okay? I'll stay with you. Luke is perfectly capable."

"No, Charlie, help him. With both of you working on this, you'll find the evil person that much quicker." She held his face between her palms and stared into his green eyes. "I'm serious. I'm fine. Go."

He delivered Marian back into Ma's embrace. "Take care of her." Charlie handed his car keys to Marian. "I'll be home as quick as I can."

Chapter 2

Luke drove to the Rogers' home. "Okay, this is what I know so far. Darla Jean was killed somewhere around midnight, give or take an hour or so. Obviously, she was strangled." Turning down a tree-lined street, he continued, "Our church had the armoire delivered to the shop around noon."

Charlie frowned, "You mean Father Eli sent it?"

"Yep. According to Rach, he sold it to raise money for …" Luke paused, "Now get this, for Darla Jean to buy school supplies."

"For herself?"

Luke slowed the car. "That's the house," he said pointing to a modest white clapboard house with dark blue shutters. Nothing extraordinary, it looked like many of the other homes on this street. The lawns were all trim and tidy with colorful flowerbeds. Welcoming porches with hanging swings and thick padded chairs made the neighborhood look innocent.

"Let me finish giving you the details before we knock on their door." Luke parked two houses down from the Rogers'. "The supplies were going to be for the school at the Dominican convent where Darla Jean was about to enter." He threw up his hand in the air and sighed. "That's all for now until we talk to Doc Leech about the autopsy and to her parents."

Charlie tugged his earlobe. "Sounds like she was a good girl. So what was she doing out at midnight?"

"Let's see if we can find out." Luke started the car and pulled into the Rogers' driveway.

Jason Rogers met them at the door. Reading the faces of the two detectives, he mumbled, "Oh, God, no." His eyes filled with tears and his breathing was short and shallow. He heard his wife call from another room. Swallowing, he rubbed his small pudgy hands over his face and took a deep breath. "Yes, honey, the police are here." He motioned for them to follow.

Charlie was surprised at Jason's transformation from horror-stricken father to composed husband. But when he caught a glimpse of Becky, he realized she would need her husband's strength and support.

Becky was standing in the wide doorway that led to a bright, homey living room. Her hand gripped the doorframe. After 28 years of marriage, she knew what he'd say before it was said. She prayed her intuition was wrong. "Jason," Becky pleaded. "Did they find her? She's all right, isn't she? Please tell me she's all right!" An agonized wail exploded from her as she slid down the doorframe like an overcooked noodle.

The three men rushed over, caught her before her head hit the floor and carried her to the sofa. Jason held his wife. Rocking her like a small child, he stroked her hair. His tears fell onto Becky's head. "Hush, now, sweetie. Shhh." Jason squeezed her and cradled her head against his thick neck. "Tell us…" His voice faltered. "Tell us what's going on."

Luke looked at Charlie. He inhaled deeply, wishing Charlie was the one giving them the bad news. But this was his town, his job, and his duty. Luke licked his dry lips and cleared his throat. He sat next to Jason. "I am so very sorry. We found Darla Jean's body this afternoon."

"Nooooo!" Becky's scream was muffled as she pressed her face against her husband's heaving chest. Her whole body shook violently with each gut-wrenching sob.

Jason's composure melted, contorting his face into a red, unrecognizable mess as he processed the knowledge that his baby girl was never coming home. He would never hear her say, "Daddy" ever again. His sweet baby girl was dead. Someone had taken his baby girl from him.

"What happened to my baby? Who killed my little girl?" Jason choked as his eyes darted from one detective to the other.

"She was strangled and found behind *The Antique Shop* around two o'clock this afternoon. The investigation is just beginning. But we will find who did this," promised Luke.

Charlie cut his eyes at Luke. *Don't make promises you don't know if you can keep, especially to a grieving family.*

Becky shrieked and buried her face deeper into her husband's shoulder.

Jason stroked his wife's hair. "Was she…?" His voice faded into a croaking sob.

Knowing what he meant, Luke replied, "It doesn't appear that she was."

A look of relief calmed Jason's tormented face. Tears streamed down his face as he rocked his wife.

Luke and Charlie each swallowed a bitter lump of grief that had gathered in their throats. They were silent as the Rogers grieved. Charlie knew there were no words that could soothe that raw, agonizing heartache of death. Luke stood and gripped Jason's soft shoulder. He left the room and returned with two glasses of water.

Jason looked at the water Luke set on the coffee table. He whispered into his wife's ear. "Honey, do you want a sip of water?"

"Noooo, I want my baby. I want her …," she wailed. Becky clung to her husband and stared over his shoulder at their family portrait. "Look at my baby. She's so beautiful. She's so …" Becky felt her husband tremble and gripped him tighter, afraid of what might happen if she let him go.

The shadows were beginning to overtake the room as the sun crept closer to the horizon. Charlie walked to a Tiffany lamp sitting on a reading table next to the well-used leather recliner. Pulling on the dangling chain, a soft light caressed the books neatly stacked at the base. Charlie nodded at Luke then tapped his watch prompting him to speak. "Jason is there anyone you would like for us to call?"

Jason nodded and took the tissue Charlie offered. He blotted his wife's red face. "Honey, please drink some water. I know it won't make you feel better but you need to drink something." Kissing Becky's forehead, he said to Luke, "Father Eli. Call Father Eli. Ask him to come." He then eased his wife out of his arms and handed her a glass of water.

Her hands trembled and drops of water splashed onto her lap. Staring at the wet spots, Becky remembered Darla Jean's head on her lap crying. Her tears left spots like the ones now staining her green dress. Her face knotted as she wept. The glass tilted, spilling water over her knees and onto the wooden floor.

Luke ran into the kitchen and came back with a roll of paper towels. Charlie and Jason stood Becky up and half dragged, half walked her to the master bedroom. Once in the room, Charlie stepped into the hallway while Jason took off Becky's wet clothes.

After a few minutes, Jason eased out of their bedroom leaving the door cracked in case Becky called out for him. Charlie could hear her moaning.

Luke was hanging up the phone when they entered the living room. "Father Eli will be here soon. We'll wait until he arrives." Luke held up his open hands. "Jason, I am so sorry. Is there anything I can get for you? Anything I can do?"

Rubbing his round pudgy face with both hands, Jason shook his head. He walked over to an antique secretary, opened it and retrieved a bottle of Locke's eight-year-old Irish whiskey. "Your father gave this to me a few years back. Never opened it, but I think it's time." He twisted off the cap. Picking up the empty water glass from the coffee table, Jason poured about two fingers' worth. He held up the glass toward Charlie and Luke. "Would you help me drown my sorrows?"

Luke shook his head. "I'm driving, and don't you drink too much of that stuff. Remember, Becky needs ya."

"Not much I can do for her now except … be strong for her. I'm hoping this might help give me a bit of courage." He took a small sip and groaned. Jason looked at Charlie and tilted the glass toward him.

"No, maybe another time."

Jason shrugged and dropped into the recliner. He rested his elbows on his knees, cradled the glass of amber liquid with both hands, and stared at his feet.

Charlie saw headlights flash through the front window. Glancing out of the window, he saw Father Eli emerge from the passenger side of a black and white 1956 Chrysler station wagon. He smiled knowing that Father Eli's sister, Josephine, would be at the wheel. She was Father Eli's right arm, completely devoted to her younger brother. Charlie watched the car leave.

Luke stood in the front doorway. He shook his head and whispered, "Like I said on the phone, Father, it's bad. Real bad."

Father Eli knelt before Jason and looked into the grieving man's eyes. Jason drank the last bit of whiskey and set the empty glass on the side table. His mouth opened, gasping for words as tears flooded down his face. Jason slid from the chair onto his knees and fell into Father Eli's embrace.

Charlie took out a business card and scribbled his parent's phone number on the back of the card. He touched the priest's shoulder and laid the card on the coffee table. Father Eli acknowledged the meaning. Luke placed his card next to Charlie's then put his palm on Jason's head and said a quiet prayer. He then turned and walked into the night with Charlie.

Chapter 3

Saint Fergus Catholic Church is quiet and peaceful. The only light in the church is from the bright glow descending upon the cross of the crucifixion behind the great altar and from the twinkling flames of the red and white prayer candles on each side.

I stand in the comforting dark shadows in the back corner of the church wondering what Jesus must have felt while He was dying on the cross. He must have felt so alone with all His disciples, but one, having abandoned Him. Well, at least His mother stood at His feet. She didn't leave Him all alone. Did He wonder with each stabbing pain, if they would ever appreciate all that He had done for them?

In the shadows, I close my eyes and pray for God to have pity on me and never abandon me. I beg God to never leave me alone no matter how great my sin is. In the shadows, I feel a peace calming my warring mind.

The heavy front doors of the church groan in protest as someone pulls them open. Heavy footfalls plod across the marble foyer and down the center aisle.

My eyes pop open as I strain to see who has disturbed my sanctuary and my communion with God and His Son. It is him! One of the men the dead girl used like pieces on a chess board, and always to her advantage. From the shadows, I watch the man stumble to the prayer candles and struggle to light a white one.

White because she is dead, not because she is pure. Oh, no! Everyone thinks she is a saint, Miss Snow White. Ha! If they only knew. After lighting the candle, the man falls to his knees and weeps quietly. Safely hidden in the shadows, I watch as his heaving shoulders become still and I wonder if the man has fallen asleep. Is it safe to leave my hidden refuge? But then the weeping man stands, wipes his eyes and nose with his sleeve, and staggers out of the church.

Leaving the protective shadows, I walk to the prayer candles and stand before the white candle the weeping man lit—the one for her. I want to grab it and smash it against the altar, and then grind it into dust with my dirty shoes. But that would be wrong. I sneer and lean slowly toward the flickering flame. I blow it out. The thrill of snuffing out her flame is almost as exhilarating as snuffing out her pathetic, rotten, little life.

Chapter 4

Charlie hated funeral homes. No matter how stately or serene they appeared on the outside, they held the ugly side of life, sorrow, and death. It didn't matter if the service was a glorious celebration. The person was dead. Knowing they would never be a tangible part of your life again was a dark fact that swirled around in your soul, in your mind.

The front of Smith and Sons Funeral Home was quite impressive, even in the fading sunlight. The two-story Victorian home with its wide wraparound porch was the most magnificent house in Mercy City. Families from all around the state wanted their loved one's funeral to take place here. Old man Smith joked that he had a waiting list with specific dates.

Charlie and Luke drove behind the funeral home to where the hearses parked out of sight. The entrance to the morgue, one could say, was uncommonly cheery considering what lay behind the double French doors. A bright red trumpet vine arched over the doorway and two gigantic clay pots filled with black-eyed susans and pansies stood on each side of the door. A rose and geranium-filled flower bed spanned the whole backside of the home.

Charlie and Luke squinted in the bright lights that illuminated the morgue's entrance. Luke pressed the call button and stood with his hands shoved in his pockets. "I saw that look on your face when I promised we'd catch the killer. I screwed up, didn't I?"

Blowing a silent whistle Charlie answered, "Well, yeah, but we've all made that mistake and you'll probably do it again. You can't help it. You get torn up by the grief and want to make it better by offering solace and closure by promising justice." He slapped Luke on his narrow back. "Don't beat yourself up. Okay?"

The doors swung open suddenly. Old man Smith's youngest son, Alan, stood with a somber smile. "Come in detectives. Doctor Leech and Miss Mary Grace are expecting you." Alan stood aside to allow them to enter.

Charlie watched Alan lead the way, thinking he resembled a robot with his straight posture and purposeful gait. The odor of chemicals used to disinfect the surroundings from the stench of death greeted them before they pushed through the stainless steel door. Goosebumps crawled up Charlie's arms. *I'll never get used to this*, he thought as he put on the paper booties, latex gloves, surgical mask, lab coat, and paper hair net.

Alan opened the door for them, then closed it promptly once they had passed.

A tall man with graying hair peeking from underneath the paper hair net spoke without looking up. "It's about time you two got here."

"Good to see you, too, Dylan," Charlie retorted. His pretty niece, Mary Grace, ran up to him pulling the mask from her nose and mouth, exposing a beautiful smile.

"Oh, Dad, leave Uncle Charlie alone." She stood before Charlie holding out her arms. "I would hug you but …" Mary Grace glanced at her stained lab coat.

Charlie drew the thin girl into his arms. "Like I've never had any of that on me."

"You're getting soft, Charlie. Get over here so I won't have to say the same thing twice." Luke stood next to Dylan, staring at Darla Jean's lifeless body.

Mary Grace's smile fell. "This one is really hard. I know … knew her."

Charlie pinched her dimpled chin. "I'm sorry, sweetie."

They all stood on the same side of Darla Jean as Dylan began. "Okay, let's begin with the obvious." Pointing to a narrow bruise around Darla Jean's neck, Dylan continued. "She was strangled, it appears, with the red curtain tieback that was found around her neck. Mary Grace took pictures of the bruises to compare to the rope pattern." He picked up one of Darla Jean's small hands. "There is a tiny puncture wound in the palm of her left hand. I have no idea from what. We found debris under her fingernails. Most of it appears to be her own skin." He then pointed to the scratches around the rope bruise. You see the clawing marks there. And there were some red fibers mixed in the skin, which will most likely verify that it was from the tieback used."

Raising Darla Jean's arm, Dr. Leech pointed to the horizontal lined bruising on her forearms. "See these bruises? The other arm has them as well. And look at these." He pulled up the sheet, exposing the bruises on her knees and shins. "I would say that Darla Jean was kneeling when the killer came up from behind and began to strangle her. She must have put up an awful struggle to cause this much bruising." Dr. Leech covered Darla Jean's legs.

Dr. Leech pushed up his black framed glasses and scratched his forehead with his gloved index finger. "As far as the rosary beads you found in her mouth, they were shoved in there after she died." He touched her lips then circled the surrounding area. "No bruises and no blood in her mouth from the cuts made as the glass beads were crammed in." He put his fist on his hips as he stared at the wall clock. "I would guess she was killed somewhere around midnight, give or take an hour."

Dr. Leech walked to a table with a large magnifier suspended over a stark white table. The table had plastic bags of varying sizes, each containing a piece of evidence. He picked up a glass slide and holding it under the magnifier said, "Look."

Charlie and Luke studied the red strands. "They have to be from the tieback," Luke remarked.

"Yep." Charlie picked up a clear plastic bag containing the tasseled tieback. "When you compare the fibers to this, you can see that it matches both the color and the width."

Luke rubbed the back of his neck. "Okay, so we have the murder weapon. But it could've come from anywhere. So finding the source is gonna be a problem." He stared at the rope, memorizing its details. Carefully placing it on the table, he turned to Dr. Leech. "Was she raped?"

"Well, I found semen but it appears to be consensual sex since there are no signs of violence, like tearing or bruising."

"She had a boyfriend," blurted Mary Grace. "Even though she was entering the convent."

The men stared at her. "Well, you don't have to be a virgin to become a nun. That's what she told me."

"Who is he?" asked Luke.

Mary Grace hesitated.

Charlie touched her gloved hand. "It doesn't mean he killed her. Did he know she was entering the convent?"

"Uhuh, he knew, but he understood … at least that's what Darla Jean said." Mary Grace looked at her father, then to Luke. "You know Matt Hoffsteader."

Charlie spoke first. "Now I remember why she looked so familiar. She worked at *The Steakhouse* with Matt. Yeah, his dad is an attorney."

Dylan added, "So that would likely explain where she had dinner." He picked up a folder. "Stomach contents were rare steak, potato, bits of bacon, lettuce, chocolate cake, garlic bread, and no signs of alcohol. But we'll have the results from the blood and semen in a few days." Closing the folder, he said, "We did find a few strands of hair that aren't hers. A couple of blonde ones which could be Matt's, and some graying brown hairs. We'll have the results back from those in a couple of days."

Luke sighed. "Well, we know she was kneeling when she was strangled with the tieback. Why was she kneeling? Begging for her life maybe? She had sex but was not raped. And she was dead when the rosary beads were put into her mouth. And as far as the bruises on her forearms, she must have hit them on …" Luke exhaled, "I don't know. And the person who did this may have had graying brown hair."

"Yes," agreed Dr. Leech.

Luke looked to Charlie.

"You're doing good. Keep going," Charlie encouraged Luke.

"It appears she had a date with Matt at *The Steakhouse* before she was killed. So we need to talk with him, Father Eli, since it was his armoire that Darla Jean was dumped in, and her parents, and of course Aunt Ella and Rachel since they found the body. We'll see where it leads after talking with them." Luke reached into his suit coat pocket and pulled out a business card inside of a baggie. "And we need to speak with this guy, too. Found it in her purse which was tossed in with her."

Charlie read the card. It was from *Your Ride Taxi Company*. Scrawled across the back of the card was, *Ask for Scottie.* A number, different from the taxi company, was neatly written under *Scottie*. Charlie's stomach growled reminding him that he hadn't eaten since lunch. "We should call Ma. Let her know we'll be late."

"Why not speak to Matt first, and then this Scottie character? After that, go home. We can speak with Rach and Aunt Ella while we eat," Luke proposed.

"Sounds like a plan. It's too late to go back to the Rogers' house. Besides, I don't think they'd be able to deal with us now anyway," added Charlie.

Dr. Leech took off his stained lab coat. "I think we've done all we can do here tonight. Mary Grace and I will meet you at Ma and Da's house." He tossed his gloves into the trash bin.

Luke nodded. "Let's go."

Chapter 5

"Ah, now my pet, you'll be callin' me, Ma. Me gynecologist calls me Mrs. McClung," Charlie's mother instructed a blushing Marian.

Emma snorted, "MA!"

"Well, it's true," Ma replied over her shoulder as she washed flour from her hands. "Marian, child, you're family." She patted her hands dry on a green apron that said *I Love Irish Boys*.

Sarah sighed, "Believe me, Marian. It's easier to do as she commands." She kissed her mother-in-law on the cheek, then hugged her. "You know I love ya, Ma."

Ma smiled, "Of course you do, Flower."

Rachel said, "I know," as she looked at Aunt Ella who was making a gagging face.

Marian rolled the name *Ma* around in her mind. It had been too many years since she felt the love of a mother. And she did feel like she belonged, like this was home. Feeling the love the women had for each other and for her, shyly she agreed, "Okay, Ma."

Laughing, Ma gave Marian a bear hug. "Okay, that's more like it."

"So, since I'm family, let me help y'all get supper ready. Give me something to do."

Ma put her hands on her full hips. Tapping her chin, she said, "Hmm, we've got things covered in here. So …" Her eyes flew around the room then settled on her three granddaughters setting the table. "Go check on the girls. Make sure things are placed correctly."

Marian was disappointed she couldn't help with the cooking, but she was glad to talk with the little girls. The table was impressive in length, around 13 feet she guessed. Three young girls were fussing over the Irish lace tablecloth. They couldn't agree if the sides hung equally around the table.

The oldest one stood with her hands on her hips like Ma. She was at one end of the table instructing the two younger girls to pull just a little bit more to make it straight. She asked, "Miss Marian does this look even to you?"

Marian circled the table. "Hmm, I think … yes, it's perfect."

"Finally," declared the two younger girls.

"Ma asked me to help you set the table. Tell me what you want me to do," said Marian, as she looked at each pretty little girl. "But first remind me of your names. I'm so bad with names."

The oldest one took charge. "My name is Sophia. I'm sixteen. Emma is my mom, Uncle Charlie's sister. The one with the freckles is Amy." The freckled face girl grinned and waved at Marian. "She's twelve and Sarah is her mom and her dad, Sean, is Uncle Charlie's brother. And that leaves my baby sister Emma Rose, but only Grandma calls her that. We just call her Rose. She's twelve, too."

Rose rolled her eyes. "Will you stop calling me 'baby sister'? Can't you just say 'younger sister'?" She walked over to Marian. "Ignore her. She thinks she's so grown up. We have an older sister named Mary Grace. She works with our dad because he's a doctor, and she's gonna be a nurse."

Amy pulled on Marian's hand. "Help me set the plates."

"Okay, where are the plates?"

Sophia opened an extraordinarily wide china cabinet. "Grandma said to use the good stuff." She began to pull out very fine, ornate china. "And you know what Grandma says."

Rose and Amy sighed, "Be careful, these things are family heirlooms and can't be replaced."

"These are so lovely," admired Marian as she placed the plates before each chair. She looked at the porcelain mark, *Arklow, impressive*. Then she studied the treasures in the cabinet. *No wonder Charlie knows his antiques. This house is filled with them.*

"So are you and Charlie gonna get married soon?" asked Amy.

"Amy, you can't ask questions like that," reprimanded Sophia.

"Well, I want to know and Daddy said if you have a question don't be afraid to ask. There's no stupid question." Amy stuck out her tongue.

The three girls stared at Marian for an answer. Her heart skipped a beat, but she continued to set the table. "Well, I think you would have to ask your Uncle Charlie that question." She finished the plates, "So, silverware next?"

The girls groaned collectively, "Oh."

Once finished, Marian wandered into the kitchen with the two, 12-year-olds' arms around her waist.

"All done, Grandma!"

"All right then, now. Ya didn't give our Marian any trouble did ya now?"

"Best workers ever!" Marian squeezed Rose and Amy close to her side. "So what can I do now to help?"

"Ah, sit yaself down. We're all but finished." Ma pointed to one of the padded stools at the kitchen island. "Let's have a spot o' tea or do ya prefer some coffee?"

"Tea will be fine." Marian hopped up on the tall stool. "Mmm, everything smells so good."

Ma poured the tea as the McClung women sat around the island. "So, Charlie tells me that ya met while he was at work."

Sipping the hot fragrant tea, Marian appreciated the wording of Ma's question. She felt all of the McClung women watching her. Nodding, she answered, "Yes, it was interesting the way we met, but hard to talk about considering the circumstances." She swallowed the lump of sadness that caught suddenly in her throat. But over the years she had become an expert at putting on a happy face. Smiling, she added, "But things have worked out splendidly so far. Mmm, this is the best tea."

"Ya can't go wrong with Lyons," agreed Aunt Ella, still wearing the lavender riding hat. She lifted her cup in a salute. "Marian, I'll cut to the chase. We all want your life history."

There was a collective gasp among the McClung women.

"Ella," chided Ma. "Don't be so …"

Aunt Ella cut short her sister-in-law. "Well, it's true! That's all we've been talkin' about for three months now. We all want to know about the girl that swept our Charlie off his feet."

Laughing, Marian said, "It's okay. If I were in your position I'd feel the same." Holding the delicate vintage cup in both hands, she took a sip and began. "Well, you'll be disappointed. My life is rather vanilla. I was married right after high school. Lee was a wonderful man." Her eyes glazed. Marian cleared her throat and finished the tea.

Ma refilled the footed teacup. Looking around the kitchen, Ma saw her strawberry blonde granddaughter standing close to a chrome cake safe. "Emma Rose, my dear, there are some blueberry scones there." She pointed to the container. "I forgot to put them out."

Rose removed the cover and handed the cake safe to her grandma. Rose asked Marian, "Do you know why these are called the fastest cakes?"

Sophia rolled her eyes and groaned. "Not that old joke, again."

"Let ya sister have a bit of fun. Marian, do ya know the answer?" Asked Ma.

Marian shook her head. "No, why?"

"Because before you know it, they're *scon'*." Rose chuckled at her own joke.

"Oh, that's so clever, Rose," Marian giggled and selected a scone. "These look so tasty." Biting into the light moist pastry, she moaned, "Mmm, these are wonderful."

"Mary Kathleen makes the finest scones in the county," agreed Aunt Ella. "But on with your story."

Ma clucked her tongue and shook her head at her sister-in-law's brashness.

"Not much more to add, except Lee was a pilot and died in a plane crash eleven years ago. We were married for nineteen years. He was an only child and when he died, his parents moved out of state. I haven't heard from them in years. I guess I'm too much of a painful reminder." Pausing, she took a sip of tea and continued. "I don't work anymore, but I love to read and garden. And I do volunteer work at a day program for people with special needs." Marian took another bite of her scone. "I do some baking but I've never mastered making scones. They always turn out dry." She looked at Ma. "Mind sharing your secret?"

"Ah, such a kind thing to say. I'd love to teach ya." Charlie's mother was, so far, impressed with his choice.

Amy leaned against Marian. "You have any kids?"

"No, I don't."

"Oh. Got any brothers or sisters?"

"I have one brother, who lives in England with his wife," replied Marian, then added, "Both of my parents were killed in a car accident."

Amy stroked Marian's hair. "So you're alone?"

Marian realized that she had been alone for 11 years. She only saw her brother a few times a year. And then there was Joan, who was the only person Marian had allowed into her life since Lee's death. There was Dianne, but now she was dead. A bit of sadness tinged her happiness. She looked around the kitchen at each of the McClung women. This was her family now. Hugging Amy close, Marian smiled. "No, I have all of you and your Uncle Charlie, now."

The telephone rang. Rachel ran into the living room where Da and Sean, her oldest brother, were watching TV. "I've got it," she said to the two men who sat mesmerized by the Atlanta Braves.

Rachel returned to the kitchen with Da and Sean right behind. "That was Luke. They're gonna be a bit late. Said to go ahead and start without them, but save them a bite to eat."

Da rubbed his hands together. "Well, let's eat."

"Not so fast Da," Rachel dampened her father's enthusiasm. "Luke said that Dylan and Mary Grace are on their way. We've got to wait for them. And don't forget the boys. They should be here any minute now."

Ma finished her tea. Groaning as she stood, "Ah, I'm gettin' old."

"What do ya need now, deary?" Da asked his wife as he kissed her rosy cheek.

"I need to be gettin' out the roast."

"I can manage the roast. Ya sit down and take it easy. Been fussin' around all week. Why d'ya think we had daughters?" Da looked at his daughters. "I can't believe ya girls standing around like ya got nothing to do." He set down the heavy roasting pan filled with two pork tenderloins stuffed apples and herbs.

Sean handed Da the carving set. Then he began to uncork bottles of wine.

The women calmly went into action. Sarah began to whip up potatoes. Emma sliced a crusty loaf of oat bread, while Rachel tossed spinach, garlic, and red bell peppers in a large deep frying pan. Sophia went outside and, returning with a bag of ice, poured it into three ice buckets. Each young girl took a bucket into the dining room and began filling the crystal water glasses.

Ma poured another cup of tea. "I've got some fine daughters don't ya know," she smiled.

Marian agreed. "You must let me do something. You did say I was part of the family."

"Ya got me now, child. There's a pitcher of lemon water in the refrigerator. Ya can fill the water glasses."

Marian felt a peace surround her as she listened to the family laughing and teasing one another. It was obvious they truly enjoyed being together. While Marian was pouring the water, Dylan and Mary Grace arrived. The family greeted them as if they were prodigal children.

"Marian, my dear, come into the kitchen," shouted Da.

Marian carried the empty pitcher into the kitchen and was embraced by a beautiful auburn-haired young woman. "It is so wonderful to finally meet you. Uncle Charlie just adores you." Breaking her embrace, she giggled, "Oh, I guess I should introduce myself. I'm Mary Grace and this is my father, Dr. Dylan Leech."

A tall man with graying black hair shook Marian's hand. "It's my great pleasure to meet you, Marian."

Mary Grace continued her introductions. "Emma is my mom. Sophia and Rose are my sisters. And my brothers are with the rest of the McClung boys at a baseball game."

The front door opened with a gang of boys pushing and shoving, trying to be the first one to greet Marian. The kitchen was full of noise, but a good kind of noise with playful yelling and goodhearted commands. The boys practically fell at Marian's feet.

The youngest of the boys squeezed to the front. After rubbing his palms on his thighs, he extended his right hand. "I'm James. Nice to meet you."

One by one, each young man introduced himself. Marian's head was spinning with names: John, Patrick, Ben, Jack, and Ryan. So many to remember at one time.

"All right now, go wash up. Time for supper," ordered Ma.

The women set the heaping bowls of food into silver dish rings. Everyone took their place behind a chair, Da at one end with Ma on the right. There were two empty chairs to the left of him. "You sit next to me Marian. Charlie will be sitting next to ya."

Clasping hands, Da began to say grace.

Chapter 6

"I didn't kill Darla Jean. I loved her," Matt Hoffsteader slurred. Coffee threatened to escape from the cup he was holding between his trembling hands. His mother sat next to him clutching his knee.

Attorney David Hoffsteader, his father, stood behind him. "They know that, son. They only want information that may lead to the person who did." He squeezed his son's beefy shoulders. "Understand?" David felt his son relax.

Luke and Charlie sat in wingback chairs across from Matt and his parents. Leaning forward, Luke confirmed David's statement. "Matt tell us what happened last night."

"Well, it was our last date before she entered the convent to be a postulant, after six months she'll be … would've become a novice." He choked. "I can't believe she's gone, forever." Wiping his nose with the back of his hand, Matt continued. "I picked her up at her house around 6:30. We were going to *The Steakhouse*. She called it her last meal." Matt began to sob.

Luke grunted, "Why did she say that?"

Matt took a deep breath. "Because … because she didn't know when she'd ever have steak again. You know, a big fancy meal." He drained the coffee cup but continued to grip it. "We got to *The Steakhouse* a little before seven o'clock. We took our time eating. She wanted to savor every bite." He smiled as he remembered the look on Darla Jean's face as if she were memorizing each taste and texture with every bite. "Then we …" Pausing, he glanced toward his mother and patted her hand. Matt stared at the two detectives. "I guess you already know. It's embarrassing, but we went to Miller's Grove, parked and had sex in the car."

His mother's nails dug into his knee. "I'm sorry, mom, but she wanted to … oh, it doesn't matter why now."

Luke nodded. "Was this the first time the two of you ever visited Miller's Grove?"

Matt shook his head as he studied his new Nike Air Force 1 sneakers. His mother's nails threatened to puncture his jeans.

"Then where did you go?' Luke asked.

"I took her home around eleven o'clock."

Luke scribbled the details on his notepad, Charlie did the same. "And that's the last time you saw or spoke to her?"

Licking his thumb, Matt rubbed a dark smudge from his stark white sneaker.

"Matt, I asked you was that the last time you saw or spoke to Darla Jean?"

Charlie noticed a few tiny scratches on Matt's hand as he tried to remove the smudge. "How did you get those scratches on your hand?"

Matt shrugged.

Luke looked to David Hoffsteader. "Your son can answer our questions here or at the station. You choose."

David grabbed his son's arm, yanking him away from his shoes. "Answer their questions. Now."

Matt stared beyond the two detectives; his tongue explored inside his mouth. He began to pick at something behind his ear then whispered, "No."

"What? Son, don't say anything else." David assumed the role of attorney abandoning his paternal demeanor. "Detectives, I would like a word in private with Matthew before you ask him any more questions."

Luke and Charlie acquiesced, leaving the room to chat on the front porch.

"Well, what do you think?"

Charlie answered, "Tough to say. Did you see the scratches on his hands?"

"Yep," Luke exhaled. "The boy is hiding something."

The screen door creaked as Ruth Hoffsteader stepped out. "David asked that you come in." She gripped Luke's arm as he passed. "My son is a good boy, you know that. He'd never hurt Darla Jean."

Luke patted her hand, not saying a word.

Ruth stared at the floor as she settled in a tapestry-covered armchair. David sat next to his son. "Matthew is ready to answer all of your questions."

"All right, let's begin with the last question. When you dropped off Darla Jean at her parents' house, was that the last time you saw her?" Luke held his breath waiting for Matt to speak.

"No, I mean yes, sorta in a way but not really, I guess." He picked up the now full cup of coffee and sipped. "You see, I saw her to the door, kissed her, and then drove away. But I turned around. I wanted to try one more time … to beg her to change her mind. I wanted her to be my wife, not be married to the church. For Christ's sake, what kind of life was she going to have locked away in some dank old convent?" Matt's face was red and sweat was beading on his forehead.

"So, did you talk to her?"

"No. When I got to her house, I saw her get into that taxi." He smirked, "You know the one, the taxi that pervert Scottie drives. He opened the door for her." Matt snorted, "Darla Jean got in the front seat with him. Can you believe that? She just had sex with me then she hops into the front seat with him?"

"So how did that make you feel?" Luke knew the answer.

"I was pissed! Darla Jean knows what that guy is like, what he's after. Her pretending to be all holier than thou. Saying that she loves me, but loves God more."

"What did you do about it?"

"I followed them." Matt shook his head. "Guess where they went?"

Luke and Charlie stared in silence.

"Our church, to Father Eli's church."

"And?" Luke wished the boy would just tell the whole story without having to be asked every question. Good ol' dad was probably to blame for that. *Don't tell them any more than you have to, son.*

"Scottie jumped out and opened the car door for her. She tried to pay him but he waved away her money like it was a snake. She kissed him on the cheek and said something to him. Whatever she said made him back away from her. She skipped away giggling." Matt grimaced at the memory. "He must have gotten a call because he jumped back into his taxi and drove off."

Luke and Charlie sighed heavily. They wanted to go home and this guy was dragging his feet. Charlie interrupted, "Look, son, if you tell us the whole story all at once without Luke, I mean Detective O'Sullivan having to ask you each question, we can leave you to your grief sooner rather than later. So can you do that? Do you mind Mr. Hoffsteader, instructing your son to do that?"

"Matthew tell them everything like you told me."

"I caught Darla Jean right as she opened the door to the church. She wanted to know what I was doing. If I was spying on her." Matt scratched his head. "I said no, that I wanted to talk with her." He shook his head. "Then she tells me that there's nothing to talk about and gives me her flirty little smile. Like that should appease me." Gulping his coffee, he choked and began to cough.

Ruth appeared next to her son with a glass of water and rubbed his back as he drank away the cough.

Matt thanked his mother. Running his fingers through his hair, he continued, "She turned away from me to go inside. So I grabbed her hand." He chuckled, "Darla Jean turned on me like a cat. That's how I got these scratches. I'm glad I backed away or she'd have clawed out my eyes. God only knows what got into her. I'd never seen her like that." Matt's sad smile contorted as tears filled his eyes. "That look on her face … like a demon. I ran back to my car and left. That's the last time I saw her." He started to cry, "I swear I didn't harm one hair on her head. I swear! I loved her … loved her." Matt collapsed into his mother's arms.

David Hoffsteader stood and motioned for the two detectives to follow. Once outside on the porch, Mr. Hoffsteader lit a cigarette. "Well, I think you can rule out my son as a suspect." Smoke puffed from his mouth with each word.

Charlie looked questioningly at Luke. He shrugged and waved away the smoke. "Mr. Hoffsteader, did you see your son return last night?" Charlie asked.

"My son is twenty-two years old. I don't keep tabs on him." Mr. Hoffsteader turned his back and walked to the end of the porch.

"So, that would be no."

Through slitted eyes, Matt's father considered Charlie. "I know your reputation, McClung. You always get your man, but my son is not the one you should be questioning."

Charlie tugged his ear. "Is that so? Well, he seems to be pretty ticked at Darla Jean for a variety of reasons. Love kills sometimes."

David Hoffsteader tossed the cigarette into the yard and with three long strides was nose-to-nose with Charlie. From behind, Luke seized Hoffsteader's elbows.

"I'd be careful if I were you, Hoffsteader," Luke hissed into his ear.

Charlie grinned. "It looks like Matt inherited his temper from dear old dad. Wouldn't you say, Luke?"

David Hoffsteader held his breath as he stared at Charlie. Relaxing, he apologized, "I'm sorry. I know better… it's just so … God, I never dreamed I'd ever be on this end of an investigation." He shook his head. "I know my son is innocent. He's got to be … just got to be."

Luke released Hoffsteader's trembling arms and helped him into a chair. "I don't understand. How could this happen? It just can't be my son. It can't!" Hoffsteader looked at Charlie and Luke. With a sad laugh, he said, "A thousand times I've heard clients say the same thing and wondered if they really believed what they said, or if they just wanted to believe it."

Charlie leaned on the porch rail. "Well, what do you really believe?" he asked softly.

Hoffsteader held Charlie's eyes. "I believe in my son. I believe he's telling the truth."

Luke patted Hoffsteader's back and looked to Charlie. "We may have more questions. Here's my card, and if …"

David Hoffsteader tucked Luke's card into his shirt pocket. "Yeah, yeah, I know the drill."

Chapter 7

Charlie didn't want this. He wanted to be home surrounded by his family as they fawned over Marian, the love of his life. But instead, he had put himself firmly in the middle of a murder investigation. He looked at Luke as he backed down the Hoffsteader's driveway and asked, "So, what do you think? Do you want to handle this one on your own?"

Luke snorted, "I know you're on vacation but the truth is no, I don't. I need your wisdom, your tricks of the trade." He turned down Main Street heading to his in-laws' home.

"Look, Luke, there's no point in hunting for any more suspects tonight. Now, tell me why I would say that." Charlie grinned, "It's a test."

Luke mulled over his brother-in-law's question. "You don't think Matt killed Darla Jean, do you?"

"Nah, but he was being a bit cagey, could be because he has a defense attorney for a dad. For now, I would keep Matt on the list simply because he has motive and opportunity. Never forget 'the one you least suspect' rings true sometimes."

Luke scratched his chin, "Well, let's see, this is a small town and I know everyone. Gossip is rampant, as you know. No one has left town and there are no strangers in town either. The murder was brutal and the rosary beads shoved in Darla Jean's mouth would say it was personal, maybe even revenge. That it was someone who knew her." He paused and looked for confirmation.

"Keep going."

"And, and, and …" Luke groaned.

Charlie snorted, "Remember K-I-S-S."

"What? Luke thought about Charlie's acronym. "All the suspects are here. We need to let her parents deal with their grief. I'm hungry and tired and can't think straight until that's remedied. Besides, it's too late to be banging on doors."

"Bingo!"

♣

Rubbing his full belly, Charlie leaned away from the dining room table and held Marian's hand resting on his knee. "Well, Ma, you outdid yourself."

"Tah," Ma clucked. "'Twas nothing son, but I'm glad to see ya eat. Our Marian here eats like a bird except when it comes to scones." Ma winked with a sly grin.

Marian's laughter floated around the room. "Well, Ma, you found my weakness, perfectly baked scones."

Charlie gaped at Marian and Ma. "What's this now, you calling her Ma?" he teased.

Ma walked behind Marian and wrapped her arms around her, kissing the top of her head. "And shouldn't she be calling me, Ma? She's family now."

Marian blushed and welcomed Ma's sincere affection.

"Oh, is she?" Charlie looked around the table. All of the family was focused on them as they agreed with Ma. "Well, then maybe I should make her a proper member of the family."

There was a collective gasp, then silence.

Marian could hear her heart pounding in her ears as Charlie took her left hand turned it over and kissed her palm. He then placed it over his heart. "I think you know this belongs to you."

Her eyes locked with his and whispered, "Yes," as she placed his hand over her heart, "and so mine belongs to you."

Like one of his tissues, a ring appeared. Charlie held the ring at the tip of her ring finger. "Would you like to be buried with my people? Would you like to hang your washing next to mine? Marian, what I'm saying is, will you marry me?"

Holding her breath, she glided her finger through the ring and with a big exhale said, "Yes, oh yes!"

Charlie pulled her close and gently kissed her. He heard pounding on the table, hands clapping, and the girls squealing, "Eeeee, there's gonna be a wedding!" The sounds of chairs scraping across the floor and feet hurrying his way, then the weight of his family descending upon him and Marian.

Da shouted, "This calls for a celebration!"

Charlie knew this meant bringing out the good Irish whiskey, Bushmills 21-year-old single malt. Da poured out a round for the adults. The younger ones pleaded for just a taste.

"Ah, surely lettin' the young'uns dip in their pinky to be part of the celebration won't be of any harm?" Da offered his glass to Patrick, his oldest grandchild. "Never hurt any of you."

With the little ones having a drop of whiskey on their pinky, the glasses were raised to toast Charlie and Marian. "It took a while, but our Charlie found the best. To Marian and Charlie! May they have a happy and solid life together."

"Oh, gross!" Rose reached for her water glass. "Tastes like kerosene smells." She screwed up her face and stuck out her tongue.

Marian handed her glass to Charlie. "I think you appreciate this more than I do."

Ma chuckled. "Aye, it's an acquired taste. Come with me, love, to the kitchen for tea and scones. We've a weddin' to plan."

Marian was ushered into the kitchen by the McClung women. Over her shoulder, she looked to Charlie, who shrugged and tossed her a kiss.

The men sat down at the end of the table. "Well, son, ya finally found the one your granny said was waitin' for ya. Aye, Marian's a fine lass indeed."

"Yep, Da, I knew it as soon as I laid eyes on her." Charlie smiled, "Strange that you should meet her the same way I did, during a murder investigation."

"About that, ya got any leads?" Da looked to Charlie and Luke.

Charlie nodded to Luke, "It's your investigation."

"Well, she was strangled and there were no signs of rape, right Dylan?"

Dylan tipped his tumbler in agreement. "Right, you know everything I know."

"The boyfriend could be a viable suspect, but you never know what may turn up. Charlie and I have a few more people to question."

Da sipped the whiskey, his eyes darting between Charlie, Luke, Sean, and Dylan. "We can't ignore the giant gorilla in the room, boys. What role does Father Eli play in all of this?"

Luke emptied his glass and went into the kitchen returning with Rachel, Aunt Ella, Ma, Sarah, and Marian. "I only wanted Rach and Aunt Ella but you know how women travel in packs."

Ma swatted Luke's behind. "Respect your womenfolk. We'll be easier to live with."

"That's enough of that, sit down, the lot of ya. We've a murder to solve," ordered Da. "Luke, Charlie, which of ya is gonna lead the investigation?"

Luke answered, "It should be me. It's my job but …" He looked to Charlie. "I'm not too proud to ask for help. This is my first murder. I can't even remember a murder happening in Mercy City. There's no one here to turn to for help. No offense intended, Da, but Ma's had you all to herself for seven years now and I don't think she'd want you going after a murderer."

"Aye, ya got that right," agreed Ma.

"And Sean, I don't think the FBI would like you spending time on this case."

Sean shrugged, "Yeah, but if you need any … well, you know what I mean, just ask."

"Charlie, it's been years since you worked in Mercy, but you still know these people. You've solved dozens of murders in Richmond. So what I'm saying is, I really would like for you to take the lead."

Marian squeezed Charlie's forearm. "It's all right. I know it's what you want to do. Besides, our family will take care of me." She gazed at her new family and grinned. "We've got a wedding to plan, don't we now?"

Charlie laughed. "Oh, so I have no say in the wedding plans?"

"Tah, do ya really want to be plannin' the weddin', makin' decisions on flowers, color schemes, and such?" asked Ma.

Reaching into his pocket, Charlie pulled out his wallet and tossed it to Ma. "Here, this is all you want anyway. Just tell me when and where. Deal?"

Ma nodded, "Aye, a wise son indeed."

"If ya want to stay in here, there'll be no more weddin' talk. We're solving a murder or did ya forget about that already?"

Silence. No one dared to argue with Da. "Only adults are allowed and only if you can add to the discussion." Out of the ten kids, only Mary Grace and Jack stayed, the rest of the kids finished cleaning the kitchen.

Da began, "Rach, Ella, tell us what ya know about this armoire and what Father Eli's got to do with it.

Aunt Ella nodded toward Rachel. "Well, Da, Father Eli called Monday morning. He wanted an estimate on the armoire, the one Darla Jean was found in. He wanted to sell it. The money was going to be donated to the school at the convent Darla Jean was joining."

Ma gasped. "I knew I had seen that armoire before. It's his granny's! How could he sell it?"

"Aye, Father Eli said it was God's will. He praised his sister's devotion to God." Aunt Ella clicked her tongue.

Ma shook her head, "How's his sister takin' it? Poor Josephine, she cherished the thing."

Aunt Ella took off her hat and fluffed out her graying curls. "When I got to the church, Josephine was nowhere in sight. The armoire was empty and had been moved out of her bedroom. It was in the left side foyer."

"So, how much is it worth?" asked Charlie.

"Twenty-two thousand, give or take a few," Aunt Ella answered.

"Get outta the garden!" Da shouted.

Charlie tugged his earlobe. "So, why was he so willing to sacrifice his sister's prize possession for Darla Jean? There's not more to tell between the two is there?" He was thinking of Matt's revelations about Darla Jean.

"She's a good girl, gonna be a nun. And Father Eli's a saint of a man. There'll be no such talk in this house, son." Ma waggled her finger at the men. "I'll be in the kitchen havin' tea." She looked at her sons. "Are ya finished with Ella and Rach?"

"For now," replied Luke.

The two women stood to follow Ma. Rubbing Marian's shoulder Ma said, "I know ya wantin' to be with Charlie, that's fine child."

After Ma was out of earshot, Da whispered, "I guess there's something amiss with Darla Jean's sanctity."

Luke sighed, "Let's just say her Mr. Hyde-side is being revealed."

Leaning forward, Charlie rested his forearms on the table. "Well, until we question everyone, I'd say we need to keep Matt on the suspect list and as much as I hate to say it, Father Eli as well. Also, the cab driver and, by the way, why did Matt call him a pervert?"

Luke smirked, "The guy is new in town. Less than a year now, I guess. Anyway, the young girls seem to think he's a hunk. They call him Scottie the Hottie. Maybe Matt's jealous?"

Charlie laughed, "Scottie the Hottie, you've got to be kidding me."

"Well, is he?" Marian asked.

"What?" Charlie blurted.

Marian blushed. "Well, there's a reason they call him that. Have you ever seen or heard of any questionable behavior from Scottie the Hottie?"

Luke shook his head. "No, but you're right, Marian. Now that this has happened, I think we should definitely take a look at him."

"Mary Grace, have you heard anything about Scottie?" Luke asked.

"No, just that a bunch of girls seem to think he's a prize. He is very nice and cute, I guess. Not my type, too old."

Luke looked to Sean who nodded knowingly. "And let's not forget about the delivery guys. Maybe one of them dumped her in the armoire. Or at least noticed something. Who knows who else we'll find once we start digging around." Luke groaned, "Man, this is getting complicated."

Chapter 8

Charlie tapped lightly on the bedroom door. Marian was sharing his sister's old bedroom with Aunt Ella, who was too spooked to go home alone. He heard footsteps. Marian slipped out into the hallway wearing a long pink billowy nightgown and robe. Her hair looked as if she had quickly finger-combed it. Goosebumps danced up his back. *Man, she's beautiful, even first thing in the morning*, he thought.

Smiling, she kissed his stubbled cheek. She hugged him and whispered in his ear, "Once I brush out the morning breath, I'll give you a proper kiss." She kissed his ear. "What time is it? It's still dark outside."

"Five o'clock. I wanted to have a little time alone with you." He took her hand. "Come on, I'll make you some coffee and maybe some breakfast," Charlie said with a wink. "Walk softly, Ma's got ears like a bat."

Once in the kitchen, Marian sat at the island while Charlie quietly made a huge pot of coffee. "You know, Charlie, I feel at home here. It's been a long time since I've felt a sense of belonging." Marian stared out the kitchen window. She could see a few stars refusing to relinquish their place in the sky. "I've missed so much but then again …" Marian didn't want to cry even though she did feel sorrow for the years she had drifted alone. She was happy, truly happy. "But I have to look at that time alone as a healing, a time to prepare myself to be able to accept this wondrous gift. You and all you bring with it."

Charlie grinned and wrapped his arms around her. "I don't care about morning breath." His gentle kiss grew more passionate as she slid her arms around him.

"I'd say get a room but ya not properly wed just yet, and I'll not be havin' any improper relations under my roof," Ma chuckled. "But I do like to see ya happy, son."

Charlie whispered, "So much for the alone time."

Marian giggled and kissed his neck.

Releasing Marian, Charlie gave Ma a peck on the cheek. "And good morning to you too, Ma."

She patted her son's cheek and kissed Marian's. "Good morning, love. Did ya sleep okay? Ella didn't snore all night did she?"

"Mmm, just a little but I was too tired to let it bother me." Charlie handed her a cup of coffee.

"Well, son, I'm glad I taught ya proper to be takin' care of ya lass." Da joined the morning party. "Now get ya poor ol' Ma and Da a cup o' caife." He kissed his wife and settled next to Marian. "Good morning, my dear."

Charlie handed Ma a cup and said, "Sit Ma, I'll make us a full breakfast. Da can help."

"Aye, carry on, son." Ma pushed her husband, "Go on then. Marian and I will need our strength." She kissed Marian's cheek. "We'll be goin' to town. I hav'ta show off my new daughter. Lots o' places to go and people to see."

"Aw, you're so sweet, Ma. I feel like the luckiest woman in the world." Marian wrapped her arms around her new ma and felt at peace.

♣

Marian picked up the almost clean plate. "If I ate like this every morning, I'd have to work out three times a day." She exhaled heavily, "Man, two eggs, bacon, sausage, potatoes, toast, coffee, and orange juice will last all day. No lunch for me."

"Tah, ya don't eat enough to keep a wee little mouse alive. Skin and bones is what ya are," fussed Da.

"I'll take that as a compliment." Marian picked up all the plates and loaded them into the dishwasher.

Luke walked through the back door. "Well, Charlie, are you ready to hit the suspect trail?" He kissed Ma on the forehead. "Got any coffee left?"

"Aye, son, take a seat and I'll get ya a cup. Have ya eaten'?" Without waiting for a reply, Ma set a plate of food before Luke. "Eat! Gotta have sustenance."

"I'll never turn down a second breakfast."

She ordered Charlie and Marian upstairs to get dressed for the day. "And wake ya Aunt Ella," Ma yelled after them. Sitting next to Luke, she questioned him. "Ya don't really think Father Eli had anything to do with this, do ya now?"

He cocked his head to one side and swallowed. "Ma, I have to be honest with you. Darla Jean was last seen going into the church. We'll have a better idea once we question him."

Charlie walked into the room. "Now Ma, don't you go playing detective when you're out with Marian, today. This is serious. Understand?"

"Tah, in all these years have ya ever seen ya Ma sticking her nose where it doesn't belong?

"No. And that goes for you too." Charlie turned and pointed at Marian.

She gasped. "How did you know I was behind you?"

Luke laughed. "In this family, they all have ears like a bat. You never quite get used to it, either." He wiped his mouth as he stood. "Let's go, Charlie."

Chapter 9

"Who should we question first?" Luke asked as he started the car.

Charlie studied his watch. "Still rather early to question Darla Jean's parents. Father Eli should be finished with the six o'clock mass."

"To church it is." Luke turned into the Dunkin' Donuts lot. "Sorry, I need more coffee."

"Make it three. We'll give a cup to Father Eli. I remember him liking it."

They were walking into Saint Fergus Catholic Church within five minutes of buying the coffee. Father Eli was kneeling at the prayer candles. Most of the lit candles were white. Charlie wondered if they were all for Darla Jean as he and Luke sat on the back pew and waited for Father Eli to finish his prayers.

Charlie looked around the sanctuary. There were dark shadows everywhere, even with the sun filtering through the stained glass windows. A person could melt into the darkness, becoming one with it. He wondered what Darla Jean saw when she entered. Did she see security and solace in the gloom? Why did she come here so late at night? Was it forgiveness she was seeking or something more tangible? Was it God's or Father Eli's love she needed?

Charlie's thoughts were interrupted by the sound of Father Eli's footsteps echoing on the marble floor. The priest usually appeared to be in the company of angels who were encouragingly patting him on the back and whispering funny jokes in his ear. But this morning those angels must have abandoned him.

Luke handed Father Eli a large cup of coffee. "Thank you," he mumbled without a smile. He sighed after taking a deep gulp. "I truly need this today." He cleared his throat. "I guess you're here to question me about Darla Jean?"

"Yes, we are. Do you want to stay here or go to your office?" Charlie asked.

Father Eli turned and said, "My office. There has been a steady flow of people lighting candles and praying. I don't want us to disturb their tranquility."

His office was dark despite Father Eli turning on the floor lamps. The heavy tapestry drapes were drawn. He pulled back the curtains letting the sunlight filter through the 12-foot windows. Only a minute amount of dust danced in the sun's rays and the rich wood paneling gleamed.

Their footsteps were silenced by a thick Persian rug. Charlie marveled at his neat and orderly office. Josephine, Father Eli's sister, must be an obsessive cleaner. He and Luke sat in the two King Louis XVI chairs placed in front of a massive, curved, burl oak desk. To Charlie's surprise, Father Eli lifted the cumbersome, tufted leather chair from behind his desk with ease and set it in front of their chairs. He sat and waited for their questions.

"Well, Father, it's good to see you again. I wish it were under different circumstances," Charlie began.

Father Eli nodded, "Yes, I wish that too, son. I wish you were here to tell me about the future Mrs. Charlie McClung." He stuck out his hand. "Congratulations on your engagement. I know Granny McClung is dancing a jig in Heaven."

"Aye, that she is," agreed Luke.

Charlie remembered how news traveled at warp speed in this tiny town. "You'll meet Marian later in the day. Ma is showing her around town today."

"It'll give me something to look forward to today. I need some cheering up." Father Eli sat back and appeared to have his band of angels back around him. "Luke, you and Charlie go ahead with your questions about Darla Jean."

Charlie went straight in, "Why did Darla Jean come here the night she was murdered?"

"She wanted me to hear her confession and be absolved of her sins."

"Hmm, when was her last confession before last night?"

"She made confession every day."

Startled, Charlie leaned forward and tugged on his earlobe. "Every day? Isn't that a bit unusual? I mean, Darla Jean didn't appear to be a sinful girl on anyone's account."

Father Eli chuckled, "She took to heart Matthew 24: 42-51 and Luke 21: 34-36. She wanted to be ready."

Luke and Charlie stared into space as they recalled the scriptures.

Charlie replied, "Thief in the night. I see, but every day?"

"Darla Jean didn't think any sin was too small, no degrees, sin was sin."

"But she was having sex with Matthew Hoffsteader," blurted Luke.

Father Eli nodded knowingly. "That's why she was entering the convent. She knew her weaknesses and wanted to be removed from temptations."

Squeezing the back of his neck, Charlie sighed heavily. "I know confession is sacred. But she's dead, brutally murdered. So tell me, was Matthew her only lover?"

Father Eli shook his head. "That I don't know. The first time she had improper relations, she let Matthew's name slip out by accident. I know because she apologized and asked forgiveness for saying his name. After that, she would only say she had improper relations."

Charlie was thankful that the priest spoke freely about Darla Jean's confessions. "Can you tell us about how long ago she began to have improper relations?"

"Eight, nine, maybe ten months ago?"

Luke scribbled all the information in a small notebook. He asked while writing, "Why were you so willing to help her? You know, sell your family heirlooms?" Looking directly at Father Eli, he asked, "You weren't one of her lovers were you?" Hearing Charlie cough and Father Eli's slight gasp, he added, "Sorry for being blunt, but it is a question we have to ask."

"It's all right." Father Eli rested his elbows on the chair's arms. He raised his hands to his mouth and with steepled fingers as if in prayer, he continued, "No, I was not. She was like a daughter to me, or younger sister, who turned to me for guidance."

Charlie noticed a few bruises on the priest's wrists. "How long had she been seeking your guidance?" He was relieved that Father Eli understood Luke's zeal for the truth.

Father Eli closed his eyes. His jaw tightened and he inhaled deeply. "For as long as I have been the parish priest here, five years. Although, she only began daily confession right after she graduated college, about a year ago. She said she felt as if the Devil and God were struggling for her soul."

He stood and walked behind the desk. Taking a large daily planner from one of the drawers, he began to flip through it, stopping on various pages. "Around six months ago, she decided she wanted to join the Dominican order in Alabama and become a teacher. So I made a few calls. She went into their aspirant program for six weeks. After that, she decided that was the right direction for her. Even after three months away from the convent, she still had the calling. She was going to enter their postulancy program in two weeks." He picked up the coffee cup and began to drink.

"And please answer Luke's question, why sell your granny's armoire? I understand it belonged to Josephine. Wasn't she upset?" asked Charlie.

Father Eli tossed the empty cup into the trash. "I wanted Darla Jean to have everything she needed to make the transition easier from having a life of plenty to a more frugal one. Teaching is hard. Can you imagine how difficult it would be not having the supplies you need?"

He returned to the leather chair. "Josephine understands the hardships of serving our Lord. She does so with much grace. My sister is my rock."

Ignoring the ringing telephone, Father Eli said, "Josephine will get that." Sure enough, after the second ring, the phone was silent. "So are there any more questions?"

"How did you get the bruises on your wrists?" asked Charlie.

Father Eli looked at the bruises as if it were the first time he had seen them. "I guess from moving the armoire. It was rather cumbersome. Henry the gardener and his son, Leon, helped me move it to the foyer so the delivery men could pick it up whenever their schedule allowed. They were doing it for free."

"So no one knew exactly when it would be picked up?"

"No, they said they would pick it up no later than today, Thursday."

There was a polite knock on the door.

"Come in," commanded Father Eli.

Josephine stepped in and stood erect with her hands clasped. "Good morning, gentlemen. I apologize for interrupting, Eli, but the telephone is for Detective McClung or Detective O'Sullivan. The caller, Dr. Leech, wasn't specific," she said with a strained smile.

Charlie was amused at how prim and proper Josephine presented herself. Ma gladly accepted Josephine's invitations to tea. She laced the tea with a few drops of brandy and always offered the most exquisite rum cake.

Father Eli handed the phone to Luke as his sister seemed to evaporate from the room.

Luke's jaw dropped. "Are you sure, Dylan? You're absolutely positive about that?" He hung up the phone and shook his head. "Darla Jean was pregnant."

Chapter 10

Charlie heard a gasp from the other side of the door. Josephine was eavesdropping. Father Eli grew pale and dropped his head into his hands. "Why didn't he tell us that last night?" Charlie wondered aloud.

"He said once he found evidence of Darla Jean being sexually active, he didn't cut open her … well … her womb just in case she was pregnant because he didn't want to upset Mary Grace. So he went back this morning and found a tiny fetus. Darla Jean was about eight weeks along." Luke blinked and scratched his chin.

"Well, this puts a new twist on things. Father, did you know about this?" Charlie asked.

Father Eli stared at the cross hanging above the office door. "No," he whispered and cleared his throat. "No, she never even hinted at it."

Charlie wondered what was going through Father Eli's mind. "Is there anything you want to tell us? Anything, no matter how insignificant you think it may be?"

He shrugged and took a deep breath. "No, I can't think of anything right now." Father Eli stood. "I need to pray."

"Just one more question. How would that have affected Darla Jean entering the convent?" Charlie asked.

"I don't know. Talk to Josephine. Now, if you will excuse me."

Father Eli closed the doors behind the two detectives. Turning off the lights, he lit a candle and then pulled the curtains together. He found the darkness welcoming and soothing. Staring at Jesus on the crucifix above the door, he fell to his knees and prayed.

♣

Charlie and Luke stepped into the hallway. Charlie saw a flash of Josephine's flowing skirt disappear around a corner. "This way, Luke."

They found her in the kitchen filling a sink with sudsy water. "Excuse me, Josephine, we need to ask you a few questions." Charlie's voice made her flinch.

She turned and scowled. "About what? Darla Jean?" Josephine's attention returned to the sink and she began to wash several coffee mugs and pots.

Luke punched Charlie in the shoulder and mouthed, "What's her problem?"

Shrugging, Charlie continued, "Yes, that's right. When was the last time you saw her?"

Josephine kept her eyes on the sudsy water. "The night before last. Darla Jean arrived earlier than usual. I was straightening the hymnals in the pews. People never put them back correctly," she growled. "I didn't see her last night. Even though Eli came into my room and told me she was praying in the sanctuary and to check on her in fifteen minutes. But Darla Jean wasn't there when I looked."

"What time was that?"

"I would say around 11:30 or so." Josephine flung water from her hands and dried them with a few paper towels. She turned and smiled sweetly, "Would you two like some tea, maybe a few biscuits?"

Charlie was fascinated by her abrupt attitude change. "Yes, that would be kind of you."

They followed Josephine into her private rooms and entered a small sitting room decorated with antiques. To the right of the sitting room, Charlie could see her bedroom. The wall in direct view was bare. *That must have been where the armoire sat,* he thought. Just like in Father Eli's office, the heavy curtains were drawn, but she made no attempt to open them. The room felt cozy with the help of several Tiffany lamps.

Charlie sipped the hot tea and studied Josephine's erratic behavior. "This must be Lyon's."

A slight tingle flowed through Josephine as she studied Charlie's face. *He's always been easy on the eyes,* she thought. "Yes, your mother introduced me to it."

Charlie tugged his earlobe then pointed to Josephine. "By the way, you're missing an earring." Charlie saw the pink flush drain from her face.

"Oh, how silly of me. I must have forgotten to put the other one in." Her trembling hand removed the dangling pearl earring and laid it on the coffee table. "My mind has been distracted, to say the least with what all has happened," Josephine replied with a nervous laugh. "Do you have any more questions concerning Darla Jean?"

Setting down the teacup, Charlie looked toward the bedroom. "Is that where the armoire was before you sold it?"

Josephine's face tightened. "Eli sold it for Darla Jean."

"How did that make you feel? I understand it belonged to your granny."

A sad smile settled on her face. "I agreed with Eli. I'm getting old and there's no one to inherit our family treasures. But our Lord blessed us with them so it is only fitting they be used to further His work."

"I see." Charlie was impressed how she avoided answering the question, and instead blamed her brother, Eli, for her loss. "I guess you knew of her pregnancy?"

A bright pink swooshed over her face. "Yes," Josephine mumbled as she refreshed her half-empty cup.

"Did Darla Jean ask for your advice concerning her pregnancy and how that would affect her becoming a nun?"

"She did not tell me of her condition, but I'm not surprised. She was torn between the flesh of man and the spirit of God. Darla Jean was determined to be a nun. 'To be a good girl' was how she put it."

Charlie was puzzled. "Why choose to be a nun and not a wife?"

Josephine sighed heavily. "I don't know. Somewhere along the way, she became terrified of going to hell. I guess being a wife was not good enough for her. Or maybe she felt she couldn't be faithful. Afraid she'd be an adulteress." A melancholy shrouded Josephine. She shrugged and murmured, "I would have chosen to be a wife."

"Why didn't you?" blurted Luke.

Her focus shifted from Charlie. She gave a nervous laugh. "Because of Eli. When mother died giving birth to him, I became his mother." She grunted, "Our father began to drink heavily, practically lived at the pub. He died shortly thereafter, so there was no one else to

care for Eli. No one. It's just been the two of us since." Josephine's
eyes began to pool. Standing, she tapped a framed picture of a plain,
chunky young woman holding a baby. "I mean look at me. Nobody
wanted me before he was born. Why would anyone have wanted me
with a baby in tow?" She wiped away a rogue tear. "I gave up
everything for Eli because he needed me. But now ... well ... I guess
I'm more of a housekeeper, a secretary. Anyone could take my place."
She stared at the photograph and whispered, "Even ..." Josephine's
voice faded into her troubled thoughts.

Charlie frowned. "Who could take your place?"

Josephine inhaled quickly as if waking from a bad dream. "I have
letters to the diocese that must go out today, so please excuse me. I
believe you can find your way out." In a blink, she was gone.

Chapter 11

"Well, that was a little weird," snorted Luke as he drove to the office of *Your Ride Taxi Company*.

Charlie pursed his lips and exhaled, "Yep. It was like watching 'The Three Faces of Eve' on stage." He pulled on his earlobe. "Yeah, weird stuff all around. The bruises on Father Eli's wrist, Josephine's strange behavior, scratches on Matt's hands, Darla Jean being pregnant, and who knows what we'll find with the cab driver."

Luke parked in front of the only taxi station in town. The Itzler family had started the cab service in 1920 and it was passed down to the eldest son, Theodore, in 1943. Theodore and his wife, Thelma, were legendary in Mercy City for many reasons. First of all, Theodore resembled Fred Mertz, and Thelma was a fascinating combination of Cruella DeVil and Norma Desmond. But their laughter and kindness were extraordinary.

"Charlie!" Thelma wrapped her thin arms around him like a boa constrictor. She tattooed his cheek with bright red lipstick.

"Better wipe that off your face before your woman gets a load of you," Theodore laughed.

"I take it Ma has introduced you to Marian already?" Charlie wiped off Thelma's trademark with a tissue.

Thelma looped her arm around Charlie's waist leading him to their office. "Your Ma is stopping by every shop with your Marian."

Charlie and Luke settled into a leather sofa with Theodore at his utilitarian desk and Thelma sitting on the corner of it. "You're one lucky chap," bellowed Theodore. "I'm going to guess you're not here just to socialize, are you?"

Shaking his head Charlie groaned, "I wish I could say yes, but no, it's about Darla Jean. We understand one of your cabbies may have been one of the last people to see her alive."

Thelma glanced knowingly at Theodore. "Yep, Scottie. Darla Jean always requested him. But then again, every single lonely female in town requests him." Theodore nodded in agreement.

Luke handed the bagged business card to Theodore. "I'm guessing the number on the back is Scottie's home."

"Yep, he was at her beck and call." Theodore leaned forward. "If I were her father, I would have nipped that in the bud. Scottie is too old for her, thirty-nine, right Thelma?"

"Yep. A thirty-nine-year-old man is too old for a twenty-two-year-old girl."

"So give us the background on Scottie," said Charlie.

Theodore adjusted his ever-present feathered fedora. "Well, not much to say. He's been driving for us since he arrived in Mercy City less than a year ago. Said he was from Missouri. He lives over at the Renaissance Apartments. Never had any complaints about him."

"Does he ever talk about what he did in Missouri or anything about his past?" questioned Charlie.

"I overheard him say something about someone who reminded him of one of his students. Other than that he pretty much keeps a tight lip.

Friendly enough, but just doesn't talk much unless spoken to," answered Thelma.

Charlie rubbed his chin. "Is he at work now?"

"No, he usually comes in around five in the evening and works 'til one in the morning. But he seems to be a creature of habit. Eats breakfast at Higgins' Pharmacy. Lunch and dinner at *The Steakhouse* where Darla Jean worked."

"Well, Luke, let's go to Higgins for a Dr Pepper and see if old Scottie is there."

♣

Luke pointed to a man sitting at the end of the counter chatting up a giggling blonde girl. "That's Scottie the Hottie. Looks like he does like them young."

Charlie eyed the dark-haired man. He didn't see anything special about him. Looked like someone who could play the part of a pirate in a movie. But there must be something about him women liked. Even old Dora, who was old enough to be his mother, seemed to be drawn to Scottie. Since they'd walked in, she'd wiped the same spot on the counter over and over with her eyes glued on Scottie. Charlie frowned. He'd never understand what women found attractive in a man.

Luke sat to the left of Scottie and Charlie sandwiched him in by sitting at the end of the counter to the right. "Say, Scottie, do you know who we are?" Luke asked.

The giggling girl rolled her eyes. "Can I get you two anything?"

"Two large Dr Peppers to go," replied Luke without looking at her.

Scottie rolled a toothpick between his teeth. "I've seen you around town. You're a cop," he said to Luke, then turned to Charlie and pointed with the toothpick. "Hmm, you must be that big-shot detective everyone is talkin' about. Am I right?" Scottie chuckled, "What can I do for you gentlemen today? Need a ride somewhere?"

Charlie was not amused. "Yeah, you can come with us to the police station."

Scottie's smile froze. "What? Why? I mean are you joking me?"

Charlie's face hardened. "No. We have some questions concerning the murder of Darla Jean Rogers. You can answer them here or in the privacy of the station. Your choice."

Scottie looked from Charlie to Luke then back to Charlie. He placed the toothpick on the counter and tossed a twenty on the counter. "That should be enough for my check and for these two fine, upstanding gentlemen. Keep the change." He winked with a sly grin and clicked his tongue as he pointed at the blonde waitress.

The giggly blonde held up her fist with the pinky and thumb extended to her ear and whispered, "Call me," as they headed out the door.

Charlie could have sworn he saw the glisten from a drop of drool in the corner of Dora's full lips. He shook his head in disbelief.

Once outside, Scottie leaned against the yellow cab. "My chariot or yours?"

Charlie stared at Scottie and wondered why he was so flippant. "We'll follow you to the station. You do know where that is?"

"I know this town already like the back of my hand," Scottie shrugged and slid into the cab.

The men pulled into the parking lot that the police station shared with the courthouse.

Scottie emerged from the cab wearing a pair of black sunglasses and a fedora similar to Theodore's.

"You can lose that," Charlie instructed as he pointed at the fresh toothpick between Scottie's smiling lips.

"You're the boss," Scottie smirked and tossed the offending object into the cab.

They entered one of the two interrogation rooms. Scottie looked around. "I've never been in one of these. Looks like what you see on TV. Cool." He drummed his fingers on the table.

Charlie studied Scottie. "Would you like something to drink, coffee, water, or a soda?" He didn't care if Scottie was thirsty. Charlie wanted fingerprints.

Scottie removed his hat and placed it on the table. "Well, it is a little warm in here. A Coke would be good. Thank you for asking," he grinned.

Luke left the small room and returned with a Coke and a folder. "Sean faxed this over a few minutes ago." He gave it to Charlie but held Scott's eyes. "Interesting reading."

"What?" Scottie snorted.

Charlie ignored him and began the interview. "How long have you lived in Mercy City?"

Scottie leaned back, crossing his arms. "About ten months."

"Where are you from?"

"Missouri."

"Did you drive a taxi in Missouri?"

Scottie frowned. "What's this got to do with Darla Jean?"

"Just answer the question."

"No." Scottie glanced at his watch. "Look, I need to be somewhere." He stood to leave. "I'm not under arrest. Right?"

Charlie sighed heavily. "Sit down. I'll make this short and sweet. I've got better things to do than to sit here with the likes of you."

Scottie slouched down in the chair.

Flipping open the folder, Charlie began, "It says here you were a high school teacher but left that profession after allegations of inappropriate relations with a student."

Scottie shrugged with a smirk. "Nothing happened. The girl had a crush that's all."

Charlie and Luke rolled their eyes.

"Really? She was caught on her knees behind your desk," Charlie shouted.

Scottie sat up defensively, "She dropped something. That's all!" he yelled.

Charlie pulled his chair in front of Scottie, blocking him in the corner. "Is that why your wife left you because your students kept dropping things? You like young girls don't you? Why? Because women your age know a loser when they see one? Huh? Is that why Scottie?"

Scottie slid his chair back hitting the wall. "What's any of that got to do with Darla Jean?"

"Because you were one of the last people to see her alive. Did she have a crush on you, too? Is that why she kissed you? What else did the two of you do?"

"What? Nothing! I mean, yeah, I guess. I don't know!" Scottie rubbed off the sweat trickling down the back of his neck. Closing his eyes, he inhaled deeply. He sighed, "Look, it's not my fault women are drawn to me."

Charlie coughed. "Women? The "women" are young enough to be your daughters."

Scottie stared off into space, completely missing Charlie's point.

Charlie looked to Luke then back to Scottie. "You've got a problem with your perception of this situation. Darla Jean was pregnant. Did she tell you that the last time you saw her? Is that why you killed her?"

Instantly, the color drained from Scottie's face. He licked his lips, "Now look, I didn't kill her. I swear. I didn't do nothing to harm that girl. I may have flirted with her, and she may have given me a kiss or two on the cheek, but I never had sex with her. Never!"

Charlie handed the Coke can to Scottie. "Tell us about the last time you saw her. Can you do that without me having to pry all the details from you?"

Scottie emptied the can and burped. "Sorry. Yeah, I, uh, got her call a little after eleven. I was just around the corner and I picked her up in about two minutes. During the ride, she talked about leaving in a few days to join the convent. She seemed happy. Eight minutes later, she was standing on the sidewalk outside of the church. I got another call so I left. I swear that's the last time I saw Darla Jean." Scottie leaned forward, "Can I leave now?"

"Why were you so close to her house?" questioned Charlie.

Scottie hunched up his shoulders. "Just happened to be there. No reason. It's a small town."

"Hmm." Charlie asked Luke, "Do you have the card?"

Luke gave the bagged card to Charlie. "This is your card. Your handwriting, right?"

Scottie studied the card. "Yes."

"So tell me, why does she have your home number? Why does she always ask for you?"

Scratching his palm, Scottie thought for a second. "Well, I guess 'cause she likes me. Well, I mean, my customer service. She had my home number, you know if she needed a ride when I was off duty."

"I see," Charlie replied slowly. "Did that happen often? Her calling when you were off duty?"

"Nah. Rarely ever. Can I leave now? I really need to be somewhere."

Charlie had no way of knowing if Scottie was telling the truth if he never recorded the fare. "Yeah. But don't go leaving town." He stood aside to allow Scottie to leave.

Luke blocked the door. With a grin he asked, "Say, Scottie, before you leave, I've got one more question. Mind if we get some blood from you?"

Scottie backed away. "What? Why do you need that?"

"So we can determine if you're the father of Darla Jean's dead baby," sneered Luke. "We can get a court order."

Scottie pushed by Luke. "I don't need this harassment. Get your court order. I'm done here."

Chapter 12

Once outside, Scottie bent forward, resting his hands on his thighs and took several deep breaths. Standing up, he strolled to his cab as if he didn't have a care in the whole universe. He drove the speed limit to his apartment and parked. Looking around the complex, he searched for anything out of place or for anyone who might be watching him.

He went into his ground floor unit and deadbolted the door. Checking the lock on every window, he pulled together the curtains denying any peeping eyes. Satisfied he was alone and hidden, he took a beer from the refrigerator and entered the room he thought of as his playroom.

Sinking to his knees, he began to weep and stare at the wall before him. Crawling to it, he touched the life-size poster of Darla Jean, the object of his greatest desire. She was his idea of a perfect woman. Scottie sat on his heels. His eyes lingered on each of the hundreds of photos of Darla Jean that covered the four walls. Standing, he meandered around touching her full perfect lips with his, running his fingers down her flawless cheek.

He sat at his desk. There was an empty soda can she had left in his cab. He put his mouth where Darla Jean's mouth had been and moaned as he tasted her sweetness left behind. Next, he picked up a card she had given him on Valentine's Day. A simple childish card that a first-grader would give, but she had given it to him. So it must have meant something. A secret just between the two of them. It was a little white, furry puppy with black, fluffy ears and big, begging eyes holding a basket in its mouth. In the basket was a big red heart that said, "For You." She was offering her heart to him. He smelled the card. Darla Jean had scented the card with her alluring perfume. He pressed the card to his broken heart, then leaned it gently against his Bible.

He stroked a silk scarf Darla Jean had dropped inside the church. Lucky for him, he had been watching in the shadows and retrieved it before that bitter old Josephine could find it. Picking up the scarf, he floated it up in the air and let it fall on his head like a veil. It was soft like her hair. He pressed it against his nose and inhaled her scent. Scottie roamed around the room looking at Darla Jean's photos through the flimsy scarf. Suddenly he stopped and glared at the photo of her outside the church. Darla Jean was sitting on a secluded stone bench. It was nestled among the trees in the garden of peace behind the sanctuary. Father Eli sat next to her. He never noticed it before but she was practically sitting in his lap.

Scottie pulled the scarf from his face. His eyes narrowed as he studied the look on Father Eli's pious face. Was that a look of lust? Why had he not seen that before? He had seen only the delighted smile on Darla Jean's face. "This is all your fault," he fumed. Darla Jean was pregnant. She wasn't the perfect angel he had envisioned. She had fallen far, far, from the heavenly pedestal he had placed her on.

Scottie held each end of the scarf and began to choke the vision before him. The ripping sound of the scarf startled him. He looked at the tattered silk and began to sob. Collapsing to the floor, he curled up into a ball and buried his face in Darla Jean's scarf.

Chapter 13

Charlie smiled. "Well, I think that went well. What do you think?"

"Yeah. Scottie was squirming in his seat. Not so hot if you ask me."

Taking one of his magical tissues, Charlie picked up the empty soda can and carried it to the evidence room. "Can you bag this, tag it, and put it with the rest of the evidence for Darla Jean? Make sure it's dusted for prints, then compare them to the ones found on the armoire."

"I'm going to start the paperwork for the warrant to get Scottie's blood," said Luke.

"I think we might as well get one for Matthew Hoffsteader and Father Eli, too. I hate to think that it was him, but in reality, he was the last person to see her alive. And a priest fathering the baby of a girl young enough to be his daughter could be enough to drive him to murder," Charlie replied.

Luke sighed, "I pray you're wrong about Father Eli. You know how devastating that would be for Ma. Well, for the whole town as far as that goes."

Charlie ran his hands over his face. "I want this over with, now."

"Look, I can handle this, Charlie. Go be with Marian."

"No, but I appreciate it. I can't be at peace until this is solved. Let's get this done and go question Darla Jean's parents." Charlie started down the hallway, then turned to Luke. "But no more murders the next time I come home."

Luke put out his hand. "Deal."

♣

Luke pulled along the curb in front of the Rogers' home. A car was backing out of their driveway. He recognized a couple from the church. Josephine's black and white station wagon was parked in the driveway. "I wonder if both of them are here," he said, pointing to the immaculate car.

Charlie groaned, "I hope they leave. We need to talk to Darla Jean's parents alone. Don't mention the warrant just yet."

"Gotcha."

A black wreath with a single red rosebud was hanging on the stark white door. It opened before they knocked. Josephine was shadowing the entrance.

"Gentlemen?"

"We're here to speak with Jason and Becky," Charlie said.

Josephine stepped back, allowing them to enter.

The aroma of a country-cooked buffet filled the small home. Charlie realized it was time for lunch when his stomach called out in response to the tantalizing smell of food.

The Rogers were sitting in the living room with their eyes closed. Father Eli had just finished a prayer.

"Amen," they all replied.

When Becky opened her eyes, she saw Charlie and Luke. She blotted her eyes with a tissue to soak the tears. Jason stood and shook their hands.

"I know this is a difficult time, but we need to ask you some questions, so we can bring you some closure," Luke said softly.

"Josephine, it's time for us to leave," said Father Eli. "Jason, Becky, if you need anything, please call me. Okay? The same time tomorrow for the rosary?"

Becky and Jason mumbled, "Yes."

Father Eli hugged them both and said, "I leave with you the peace of God."

Father Eli nodded to Charlie and Luke as he passed.

Becky smiled when she heard Charlie's stomach growl. "Come to the kitchen and let me get you something to eat."

The three men followed her willingly.

Every inch of the kitchen table and countertops was hidden by containers of food. "Jason and I will never be able to eat all of this," Becky said as she moved a couple of large platters from the table to the stovetop. "Please sit down." She took two melamine plates and filled them with fried chicken, mashed potatoes, green beans, carrot casserole, corn, and a yeast roll. "Here. Eat. I'll get you some tea, or do you prefer something else?"

Charlie didn't like the idea of Becky waiting on them hand and foot, but he knew it was a way for her to forget about her grief if only for a few minutes. "Tea is fine, thank you."

Jason started a pot of coffee while Becky continued to fuss over Charlie and Luke. "Do you need salt or pepper? Or some butter for your roll?" Becky didn't wait for an answer. She retrieved the items offered. "Oh, dear me. I forgot the napkins."

Sitting at the end of the table with a mug of coffee, Jason watched his wife flit around the kitchen. "Honey, please sit down."

Standing in the middle of the room, Becky froze with a plate of brownies in her hands. She didn't want to sit down. That meant they would ask questions she didn't want to answer. Questions which would remind her that her baby girl was never coming home.

Jason took the brownies from her and guided her to a chair at the end of the table. Becky sat still staring at the plate of brownies. "Here drink this. It's your favorite."

She looked at the glass and drank.

Charlie had seen Jason pour a generous amount of bourbon into a glass and top it off with cola.

"Can you make another, please, Jason?" Becky had finished it in two giant gulps.

Jason filled a larger glass, giving it to his wife.

"Okay, I think we're ready for your questions."

Charlie nodded to Luke.

Luke cleared his throat. "Can you tell us about Darla Jean? How she appeared the weeks before … this happened? If she acted differently or mentioned anything that may have seemed a bit odd?"

"Well, she slept a lot more than usual," answered Jason. "But other than that, she was Darla Jean as usual."

Nodding, Luke continued. "I see. Did she say anything about Matt being upset that she was joining the convent?

"No." Jason sipped the coffee. "He knew Darla Jean was determined to answer God's call."

"How did you feel about her becoming a nun?"

Jason held the warm cup and shrugged. "To be honest, I'd rather have had grandchildren, but it's what she wanted to do more than anything. Who was I to stop her?"

"What was her relationship like with Father Eli?"

"What you'd expect, a counselor, a priest. Nothing more." Jason didn't like the question. He wondered if there was something they knew that he should know. "Why are you asking that question?"

"Just getting all the facts. That's all."

Becky stood and wobbled. Steadying herself she said, "I have to show you something. Stay here. Please continue to eat." She left the kitchen.

Charlie and Luke looked at Jason.

"I don't know what she's talking about. Really, I don't." Jason looked confused and worried. He was about to go after her when she reappeared holding a small blue box with two white daisies printed on the sides.

Charlie took the box and read the words *Pregnancy Test Kit*. "So you know." He handed the box to Luke.

Tears streamed down Becky's cheeks as she nodded and finished her drink. She refilled the glass with bourbon only.

"What? I don't understand. Becky, what are they talking about? You know what? Tell me, Becky. TELL ME!" Jason yelled.

Becky grimaced as she swallowed the strong drink. Her face contorted as she tried to say the words. Then she blurted, "DARLA JEAN WAS PREGNANT!" In between gasping breaths, she moaned, "Our grandchild died with her."

Jason wrapped his arms around his wife as she howled, "Our baby is dead. Oh, God, our baby is dead." Becky's wailing turned into soft moans, then to eerie silence.

Charlie and Luke pushed their plates away barely touched. "Jason," Charlie stood, "We'll come back later."

"No," barked Becky. "No, I want some answers. I have to know who killed our Darla Jean and her baby, our grandchild." She stood and with trembling hands, wiped her wet face. "I need to go to the bathroom." Looking at their full plates, she apologized for upsetting their appetites. "Please, eat. It'll make me feel better to see you eat. Please."

Charlie picked up his fork and began to eat. "Mmm, Becky, thank you. This is very good."

She smiled. "Jason, can you help me? I'm a little unsteady."

"Sure, honey. Excuse us for a second." Jason guided Becky down the hallway.

Luke waited until he felt they would not be overheard. "Do you think Darla Jean told her?"

Charlie pushed his food around the plate. Tearing a roll in half, he shrugged, "Women seem to have this intuition when it comes to that, but who knows. We'll have to wait until they get back." He bit into the soft roll.

Becky returned refreshed, but red-faced and with a handful of tissues. "Can we continue, please?" She glanced at Luke. "You're not eating. Please eat. I know you're hungry. I heard your bellies rumbling. Eat. Both of you, now."

Charlie swallowed. "Becky, did Darla Jean tell you about her condition?"

She shook her head. "No, but I suspected it. The signs were there." Sighing heavily, she continued, "Last night, I couldn't sleep. Doing laundry soothes me. I was putting away some of Darla Jean's clothes and I found that." Becky looked at Jason. "I'm sorry I didn't tell you sooner." Tears began to spill. "I just couldn't. I just …" her voice faded away.

"Is it Matt's baby?" asked Charlie.

Becky stared at Jason. "I guess. I mean … I mean what other secrets did she keep from us?"

"How could you think that about our daughter? I'm surprised at you Becky. She was a good girl."

She laughed weakly. "Really, Jason? Darla Jean was pregnant." Becky sipped the bourbon.

Jason's jaw tightened as his hands balled into fists. He looked at Charlie. "Did Matt kill Darla Jean because she was carrying his baby? Did he?"

"That's what we're trying to find out." Charlie wiped his mouth. "Did she ever mention a guy named Scottie?"

Jason's eyebrows bunched together. "The cab driver?"

"Yes, did she ever say anything, no matter how insignificant you may think it is?" Charlie asked.

"The only thing I ever heard her say was he was a good cab driver, polite and respectful. That's all. Why?" Becky answered. "Do you think he had something to do with this?"

Charlie shook his head. "We don't know. He was one of the last people to see her." He decided to go in a different direction. "Did you see her when she got home? Did you know she was going to church for confession?"

Jason and Becky replied, "No." Becky added, "We trusted her. I went to her room around two to check on her and she wasn't in her bed. It was still made. I knew something was wrong. She's always home by midnight. Always."

"Is that when you called the police or did you call Matt's parents?"

"When Becky told me Darla Jean didn't come home, I called the police. Then I called Matt's parents. They were useless," Jason said.

Charlie tugged his ear. "So the last time you saw her was around six thirty when Matt picked up Darla Jean?"

Jason nodded. Becky began to weep quietly.

"May we look at her room?"

They both nodded.

♣

From Darla Jean's bedroom, Charlie could hear the muted sounds of Jason trying to comfort his distraught wife. He wondered who would comfort Jason. Father Eli?

"Her room is pretty vanilla, rather plain for a young girl, don't you think?" Luke asked. He looked at the few things sitting on the dresser, a camera, some lipstick, and makeup. The usual things you'd find.

"Yeah." Charlie looked at a picture spanning the length of her headboard: Jesus bathed in bright sunlight extending His right hand as if welcoming you to join him. Charlie found it very calming. On one side of the window was another picture of Jesus sitting on a large rock surrounded by children. On the opposite side of the window, a picture of Jesus praying in the garden. And another portrait of Jesus hung beside the bedroom door. It was the last thing Darla Jean would see as she went out into the world beyond her room.

"There's nothing of any interest hidden in any drawers. Nothing taped to the bottoms or back of them either." Luke ventured toward the closet. "Not many clothes either." He stood with his fist on his hips. "It's like she was living the life of a nun. No books or music, just the Bible for entertainment." Kneeling, Luke looked under the bed. "Bingo. Looks like a photo album."

The album looked fairly new. Flipping through the pages, they saw photos you would expect to see of her parents and Matt. Charlie wondered why the album was hidden under the bed. And there it was. A picture of her with Scottie the Hottie sitting on a blanket. There were more pictures of them. They all appeared to have been taken on the same day. Darla Jean and Scottie looked … in love. Charlie continued turning pages. The last few were mundane pictures of Father Eli.

Charlie closed the album. "Looks like Darla Jean was confused about what she wanted. Was it Matt, Scottie, Father Eli, or Jesus?"

"According to Father Eli, Jesus won."

Charlie nodded. "So who is the father of her baby?" He stared at the portrait of Jesus. "Have you noticed that the pictures she has hanging on the wall resemble Father Eli?"

"You think she was trying to have her own son of God through him?"

"I don't know what to think except she's not the girl everyone thought she was." Charlie carried the album with him. "Let's tell her parents we're taking this with us. Does that camera have film in it?"

"Yep."

"We'll take that too and get the film developed."

They returned to the kitchen. Becky was clutching the half-empty glass of bourbon and Jason was massaging her bunched-up shoulders. Neither Jason nor Becky noticed them enter the quiet room.

"We wanted to let you know, we're taking a photo album and a camera from Darla Jean's room. We'll return them as soon as possible."

Jason replied, "Sure, take whatever you need."

"All right, we're leaving. We can show ourselves out." Charlie and Luke turned to leave. Charlie paused. "I have one more question. Did Darla Jean own a red glass beaded rosary?"

"I don't know," mumbled Jason.

Becky sighed heavily, "Father Eli gave it to her."

Chapter 14

"Hello, Mary Kathleen! I heard your son was visiting. And he has a girl with him," greeted Doreen Butler, a regular customer of *The Antique Shop*.

"Aye, that he is." Ma hugged the petite lady with perfectly coiffed graying blonde hair.

The brass doorbell chimed as Marian pushed open the door. She waved at Aunt Ella and Rachel standing behind a glass display case.

"That's Charlie's girl, Marian. Isn't she a fine thing?" Ma smiled, proudly waving her over. "Come here, my child." Ma slipped her arm around Marian's waist. "I'd like for ya to meet a good friend. This is Doreen, one of our best customers I might add."

"It's such a pleasure to meet you, Doreen. This is my first ... well, the first chance I've had to look around. So many lovely things." Marian softly clasped the older lady's hand. "Where do you recommend I start?"

Doreen grinned. "My favorite hunting ground is here." She placed a hand on the glass display. "You can't go wrong with jewelry."

Marian marveled at the exquisite pieces sparkling under the bright lights. "Oh my, Doreen, you are absolutely right." She concentrated on the dangling earrings. "I really like these four pairs."

Aunt Ella stuck her hand in the case. "These, love?"

Marian breathed, "Yes."

"Oh, good choice, Marian," Rachel commented. Doreen and Ma clucked in agreement.

Laying the four pairs of earrings on a blue velvet cloth, Aunt Ella detailed each one. "Ah, ya must be part gypsy, my pet," she said as she touched the delicate filigreed pair. "These are eighteen karat gold. And this pair is sterling silver tribal birds. Now these two pairs, ah, these are top shelf." Aunt Ella held up an art deco sapphire, diamond, and pearl dangle earring. "This pair is six thousand dollars and these …," she held up the pair with south sea pearls, diamonds, and platinum dangles. "These are eight thousand dollars. They would look absolutely stunning on ya. Stunning I say."

Marian gasped. "I had no idea I had such expensive taste." Clearing her throat, she touched the sterling silver pair. "Can I afford these?"

Ma clicked her tongue. "Everything is affordable, depends on how deep in debt ya wanna go."

"Oh, Ma." Rachel picked up the silver ones. "Even I can afford these on a cop's salary. They're only thirty bucks. And the gold ones aren't too bad, about two hundred dollars."

Marian smiled. "I'll take those two and dream about the others."

As Rachel and Aunt Ella boxed up the earrings, Doreen and Ma escorted Marian around the elegant shop.

"What are you going to do with the armoire?" Doreen asked.

"Ah, the buyer still wants it, believe it or not. Said he'd have the thing blessed. But we don't know how long the coppers will be hanging on to it."

"Ooo, that's the only way I'd have it in my house." Doreen shivered.

Marian giggled. "Why do you call policemen coppers?"

"Aye, that's a good question. I grew up with my granny calling them coppers. Supposedly, because of the copper badges they used to wear in the day. Just stuck. Da calls himself a copper."

"Interesting." Marian sighed, "Ma, you have the most elegant antique shop I have ever seen."

"The McClung family is known far and wide for their shop. Only the best you'll find here," agreed Doreen. She pulled Marian close and whispered, "I hear tell that even some of the high-up politicians have shopped and sold here. If you know who I mean," she said, tapping her button nose with a wink.

Ma tilted her head, shrugged, and grinned.

"Well, I have no doubt it's true. I mean this place is amazing; the quality of the pieces is superb."

"We need to be gettin' to see Father Eli and Josephine. I can't wait for them to meet you." Ma kissed Marian's cheek.

"Here's my credit card." Marian gave the card to Rachel.

"Nope, Charlie gave us strict orders. "Whatever she wants, she gets." And he's to pay for it."

Aunt Ella chimed in. "Your money is no good. Stick it back in your wallet. I don't wanna be cheesin' off Charlie."

Marian insisted.

"My child, let Charlie be treatin' ya like the lady ya are." Ma patted Marian's cheek. "He loves ya. Ya know that, hmm?"

She looked at the ring on her finger. "Yeah, I know he does." Marian kissed her future mother-in-law's cheek. "Let's go see Father Eli and Josephine."

♣

Ma softly rapped on Father Eli's doorframe. "May we come in for a wee visit?"

His head snapped toward Ma's pleasant face. "Mary Kathleen, I have been waiting all morning for you to stop by. Please come in, sit." Hugging Ma, he smiled at Marian. "You are lovelier than I had imagined. Charlie is a blessed man." Embracing her, he kissed her blushing cheeks. "I'll call Josephine to bring us some coffee."

"That'll be lovely, Father." Ma motioned Marian to sit as he asked Josephine to bring coffee.

"She'll be here directly. So, tell me when is the wedding? Will it be here, I hope?"

"My, news travels fast. Well, we haven't set a date yet but ..."

Ma cut in. "Ah, ya can't be waitin' forever, my pet. Ya both been waitin' too long already."

Marian felt a hot flash swoosh over her. "Yeah, I'm definitely not getting any younger. Fifty is staring me in the face."

Father Eli coughed. "No, you can't be more than thirty-five. I thought Charlie was robbing the cradle."

"No, Father, I'm forty-seven."

Father Eli flipped open a daily planner. Running his finger across the pages, he stabbed a day and grinned. "When are you leaving?"

"Tuesday. Why?" Marian answered hesitantly.

"Let's see, today is Thursday." He looked at his watch. "Still early." Raising his eyebrows, Father Eli announced, "Sunday looks like a good day for a wedding."

"Uh, that's a bit soon …" Marian paused.

Ma clapped her hands and chanted, "Oh, yes, yes, yes."

A coy smile played on Marian's lips. She really would like to get married soon, but Joan would kill her if she wasn't her matron of honor. An idea popped into her head. "Ma, do you think we could pull it off? I mean there's a lot to do. What's Charlie going to think?" She groaned, "Oh, I don't know."

"Hush, Flower, Charlie is gonna be fine with it. And me and my girls could have ya ready to marry today if need be." Ma laughed. "Father Eli write it down in ink. There's gonna be a weddin' this Sunday."

The sound of rattling china made the three turn around. Josephine stood in the doorway with a frozen look of disbelief.

"Josephine, please set the tray on the desk and come and meet Marian, Charlie's fianceé. They're getting married this Sunday. We have a lot to do between now and then. Pull up a chair."

Josephine swallowed and blinked several times. "Uh, yes." She smiled sweetly, setting down the coffee, "It's such a pleasure to meet you, Marian." She poured the coffee and offered pound cake. "Eli, I have other pressing duties."

"Josephine, you're being rude. Please sit."

Her face flamed. "Of course, you're right. I'm sorry." Josephine sat down abruptly.

Ma squeezed Josephine's hand. "Aye, we can't be plannin' this weddin' without ya help, love."

She grinned brightly. "Eli, hand me a notepad and pen." Josephine leaned on her brother's desk. "Sunday, you say. That works perfectly, Eli. The wedding can be right after morning mass. I know the fellowship hall is free. Is that okay for the reception?"

"Aye, that's perfect. Marian, what d'ya think?"

She hunched her shoulders. "Huh, sure, Ma, I trust you. But what kind of reception? Maybe light refreshments?"

Ma shook her head. "We'll not be having light refreshments at your weddin'. This's gonna be done right. Everybody'll be starving. We'll have a proper sit-down luncheon."

"But ..."

"No buts about it, child. Trust me. We can make it happen. Can't we, Josephine? She's the best weddin' planner for miles around."

Josephine blushed. "Well, I don't know about that, Mary Kathleen, but thank you for your confidence in me."

Marian laughed. "This is happening so fast. But Ma, can I get you to agree on something?"

"Aye, what would that be now?"

"Joan, my very best friend in all the world, will have a fit about this. I mean not being here. So when we get back to Georgia, do you mind if we have another ceremony and reception? All of you will have to be there. Can you agree to that?"

"Of course, my pet. Besides, we've been wantin' to visit Charlie's new home."

Marian jumped up and hugged everyone. "But I think we better find Charlie. We can't get married without a license."

Ma gasped. "I forgot about that." She snapped her fingers. "What about this plan? Father Eli can get a cab for you to find Charlie. Josephine and I can plan the weddin'. That's if ya trust us?"

"I don't want to stick y'all with everything." Marian had already stood to leave.

"Go, all ya have ta do is show up for the weddin'. Go on now. Find Charlie. But before you go, what're your favorite flowers, ya favorite colors?" Ma held on to Marian's wrist.

"Anything purple will do." Marian sat down. "I feel bad asking you to do all of this. I'm not so sure if this is a good idea after all."

Ma rolled her eyes and sighed. "It's settled. Josephine and I are more than capable of doing this. Make an old woman happy. Go, now."

Josephine nodded. "It's my pleasure. Do as Mary Kathleen says. Eli, get Marian a cab."

Father Eli made the call and walked with Marian through the sanctuary and then waited with her outside for the cab. The yellow cab arrived within a few minutes.

"Hello, Thelma! I'm surprised to see you driving." Father Eli held the door open for Marian. "Scottie usually comes when I call one for..." his voice faded. Caught up in the excitement of the wedding, he had momentarily forgotten about Darla Jean's death.

Thelma replied. "Yeah, well, when I heard it was Marian needing a ride, I hustled on over myself. Where's Mary Kathleen?"

"Hello, Thelma, so good to see you again." Marian slid into the car. "Ma is with Josephine."

Father Eli blurted, "They're planning a wedding this Sunday for Charlie and Marian."

"Well, holy hell! That's damn quick." Thelma's hand flew to her mouth. "Sorry, Father."

He laughed, "I'll see you in confession. Right?"

"Yep," Thelma quickly agreed. "Where to, Marian?"

"I need to find Charlie, so I guess the police station."

Father Eli watched the cab disappear. The smile eroded from his face as his thoughts returned to his dead Darla Jean.

Chapter 15

Thelma glanced in the rearview mirror. Marian was taking in the views of Charlie's hometown. She smiled as she thought how lucky Charlie was to have finally found the girl his granny had predicted was waiting for him. Thelma cherished Theodore. She didn't have to think twice when she first laid eyes on him. *When you see your true love, you know it.*

"So, tell me, Marian, how did you and Charlie meet? That's if you don't mind me asking." Thelma watched conflicting emotions struggle for control on her passenger's lovely face. A sad smile won.

"He was investigating the death of my friend and neighbor."

"Oh, I'm so sorry. I didn't mean to upset you." Thelma felt like biting her tongue.

Marian chuckled. "No need to apologize. Now that I think about it, now that it's all in the past, it was one of my worst days and one of my best."

Thelma nodded, afraid to pry anymore. "That's the police station right there."

"If I had known it was this close, I would've walked."

She stopped in front of an old stone building straight out of a 1931 gangster movie.

"It's marvelous. How old is it?"

Thelma pursed her bright red lips, "Mmm, I think it was built in the early nineteen hundreds, but the inside is thoroughly modern."

Marian handed Thelma a twenty. "Enjoyed talking to you. Maybe we could have a coffee and you could tell me about Charlie in his younger days."

Thelma pushed away the twenty. "It's on me."

"No, I insist."

"Nope."

Marian grinned, "Use it to buy us a coffee and a piece of pie when you come for me after I see Charlie."

Thelma laughed. "Kinda hard to turn down that deal." She handed a business card to Marian. "I expect to hear from you."

Marian waved as the cab pulled away from the sidewalk. She walked up the worn granite steps. Stopping under the high arched portico, Marian absorbed the sunlight filtering through the Corinthian columns. Funny, she thought, how comforting she found the building. Most people probably dreaded the sight of the police station, but this was home to the McClung clan and she was now part of them. So many years of being alone made the thought of being part of a clan exciting.

Marian pushed through the heavy doors into a small marble foyer and through another set of double doors. Inside, she was surprised to find a modern one-story building, although the front façade appeared to be a very late 19th-century two-story building. A mahogany reception station stood immediately before her. Two officers, one on the phone and the other one typing, greeted her with a smile.

"You don't have to tell me who you are, Miss," the young officer stood and extended her hand. "You have to be Charlie's girl. I'm Kitty. I mean Officer Kitty Donovan."

"Yes, I'm Marian. It's such a pleasure to meet you," she said, returning Kitty's toothy grin. "Is Charlie available?"

The other officer ended his phone call. "Marian! So good to see you, again." Sergeant Mike Purvis reached over the granite counter, shaking Marian's hand.

"Oh, what a pleasant surprise. How are you, Sergeant Purvis?"

"No, no, no." Mike shook his head. His blues eyes sparkled as he laughed. "You call me Mike."

"Okay, Mike," Marian agreed.

"Charlie and Luke are still out taking statements. Would you like to wait? Just-brewed coffee in the break room."

"Does that coffee come with stories of the old days with Charlie?"

Mike winked, "Kitty, tell Charlie we're in the break room when he returns."

"Yes, sir."

Marian spoke to the young blonde officer. "Would you like a cup of coffee? I'll be more than happy to bring it to you."

Kitty's face lit up. "No, ma'am, but thank you for asking."

Mike and Marian turned to leave.

"Excuse me," Kitty halted their departure. "Here comes Charlie, now."

"Marian!" Charlie embraced her and kissed her forehead. "Where's Ma?"

"She's with Father Eli." Marian's brow wrinkled. "Everything is fine and I know you're busy, but I have something I need to tell you, or rather ask you. It can't wait. Do you have a few seconds? I promise it won't take long."

Charlie sensed it was going to be something good. "Take all the time you need." He looked at Mike. "Sorry, pal, you won't be able to fill her with tall tales of our glory days."

Mike snapped his fingers. "Rain check on the history of Charlie?"

Marian held out her hand. "Promise with a shake?"

Shaking his head, Charlie replied, "Remember, Mike, I've got stories, too."

Mike chuckled, "See, ya later."

"Luke, I'll meet you in your office." Charlie slid his arm around Marian's shoulders and began to walk. "Let's go somewhere private," he breathed into her ear.

A shiver waltzed down her spine. She was glad Father Eli was eager to get them married. It was becoming increasingly difficult to be a good girl. Marian blurted, "We need to get a marriage license today."

Charlie kept walking. "Okay. You don't have to explain. Let me guess. Since you are here and Ma is with Father Eli, the two of them are orchestrating a wedding before we leave."

"Are you okay with that? I mean, I know you just asked me to marry you yesterday."

Swinging her into his arms, he kissed her gently. Charlie released Marian and locked eyes with her. "To be honest with you, I would like to do more than just kiss you."

Marian felt a hot flash instantly consume her. She grinned, "So, I guess you're saying the sooner the better?"

"The courthouse is next door." He grabbed her hand and almost ran to Luke's office.

"Hey, we'll be back in a few minutes. We're going to the courthouse to get a marriage license." Charlie didn't wait to hear Luke's response. He fled back down the hallway and stopped in the lobby. "We're getting married and you're all invited," he yelled.

Luke almost collided with Marian. He grabbed her shoulders from behind and asked breathlessly, "When?" as everyone within earshot began to congratulate them.

Baffled, Charlie looked to Marian.

"Oh, uh, I forgot to tell you. It's this Sunday after the eleven o'clock morning mass," Marian laughed. "Ma is planning a big reception afterward. We don't have time to send out invitations, but all of you are invited. Please tell everyone for us."

"You old dog." Luke slapped his brother-in-law on the back.

"Gotta go," Charlie shouted as he and Marian fled the lobby.

Charlie invited everyone they met on the short walk to the courthouse to their wedding. And once inside, he continued his mission to inform everyone about their wedding.

Chapter 16

Charlie's face-splitting grin evaporated as he sauntered into Luke's office. "What's the matter?"

"Theodore called. Said he's got something to show us."

"What?"

Luke grabbed his car keys. "He said it was something we had to see. Wouldn't tell me what it is."

Pulling onto Main Street, Luke said, "This must be tough for you."

Charlie smirked, "Yep, it's tough all right. Most of me wants to be with Marian, while a nagging part tells me we have to get this solved before it goes cold." He grinned. "But I've got Sunday to help me get through this."

"Yeah, I guess Ma is behind it all."

"All I can say is thank God for her if you know what I mean."

Luke nodded. He pulled into the *Your Ride Taxi* parking lot. "Ready?"

"I hope whatever Theodore has is going to help close this case."

Theodore and Thelma met them at the door. "It took you long enough."

"Hey, go easy. Charlie was at the courthouse getting a marriage license. The wedding's Sunday."

Thelma squealed and bear-hugged Charlie while Theodore crushed his hand. "I know, Father Eli told me."

"You're killing me," Charlie groaned.

"Sorry, I'm so excited." Thelma pushed them into their private office.

Charlie heard Theodore lock the door. "This must be big."

Theodore dropped into the worn desk chair and unlocked the center drawer. He handed a picture to Charlie.

Charlie exhaled slowly as he stared at the color picture. He handed it to Luke. "Where did you get this?"

"I saw a corner of it sticking out of Scottie's locker. So, I gave it a little tug and out it came." Theodore saw Charlie's frown. "Hey, they have no right to privacy here. They all know that. I tell every one of my drivers when I hire them that this is my building, my cars, so that makes everything my business and my property."

"Okay. Have you opened his locker?"

Theodore shook his head. "I wanted to see what you said first."

"Where is Scottie now?"

Looking at the Kit-Cat clock, Theodore hunched up his shoulders. "Not sure. He could be at the pharmacy, the diner, or in the park."

Thelma picked up the phone. "I'll find out." She slowly replaced the receiver. "Well, speak of the devil."

They followed her stare out of the glass-paned wall. Scottie had just parked his taxi.

"How fortuitous," Charlie remarked as he went to meet Scottie.

Scottie leered, "Officers, I thought we'd finished our business. Or are you harassing me for fun?"

"Yeah, fun," Luke sneered as he handed Scottie the picture of an almost naked Darla Jean. "Explain this."

Scottie turned crimson.

"We're gonna take a look inside your locker." Charlie gripped Scottie's biceps from behind.

He meekly walked to his locker. Luke opened it and began to remove neatly folded clothes placed on top of a pair of sneakers, sitting on top of a cigar box. Luke opened the box. "Bingo!" He looked at Scottie. "You're not too bright, are you?"

Scottie chewed the inside of his cheek and looked away.

Charlie looked at the pictures of Darla Jean. Like the one Theodore found, these all appeared to have been taken without her knowledge. "So, it looks like you had a thing for Darla Jean?"

Scottie remained silent.

Charlie tilted his head toward Luke. "Handcuff him."

"Gladly. You have the right to remain silent. Anything you say or do can and will be held against you in a court of law. You have the right to speak to an attorney. If you cannot afford an attorney, one will be appointed for you. Do you understand these rights as they have been read to you?"

Scottie nodded.

"Sure you do. It's not your first time." Luke walked him to the back of his car.

"We're going to take the box and send an officer to process the locker. Don't let anyone near it," instructed Charlie.

Thelma replied, "I'll stand guard and Theo will take Scottie's shift."

♣

Sitting in one of the interview rooms at the police station, Scottie wiped the ink from his hands. He ripped the adhesive strip from the bend of his elbow and tossed it on the table, then stared at the one-way mirror.

Charlie and Luke entered the small room.

"Well, Scottie, what do you have to say?" asked Charlie.

"I'll wait for my lawyer."

"Are you sure about that?" Luke replied.

"Yep. Got nothing to say."

Charlie tapped his fingers on the scarred table. "All right. Just so you know, we do have a search warrant for your apartment." He watched Scottie's Adam's apple bob and his jaw tighten as sweat beaded on his forehead. "Are you hot, or worried what we'll discover?"

"Got nothing to say."

"All right then." Charlie stood beside Luke. "I guess we'll find out for ourselves. Chat with you later."

Scottie stared past them as they left.

♣

"Holy cow! Charlie, you have to see this." Luke yelled as he stared at the walls covered floor-to-ceiling with pictures of Darla Jean.

"This is not good," Charlie said as he looked at the life-size poster of Darla Jean completely naked. He didn't want to think about how it got stained. "Make sure you photograph each wall and everything in this room before anything is removed."

Charlie studied the items on the desk. They all appeared to have belonged to Darla Jean or been used by her: empty soda cans, wadded lipstick-smeared napkins, a torn scarf, lip gloss, and even underwear. He wondered how Scottie had gotten the panties. "This is one perverted guy," Charlie said as he sat on the swivel stool in the middle of the room. "He could sit here and be surrounded by her."

"He took these outside of her bedroom," Luke noted as he examined various photos of Darla Jean kneeling beside her bed, undressing, and asleep in bed.

Charlie noticed a picture of Father Eli and Darla Jean. "Hmm, looks like Scottie followed her all around town. Here are some more of Father Eli and her."

Luke stood beside him. "They look rather chummy." He pointed to a few of her with Matt. "She looks chummy with everyone. I guess Scottie didn't mind sharing her."

"Yeah, but what ticked him off enough to kill her? Maybe he didn't want to be tied down with her and a baby?" Charlie tugged his earlobe. "It was all a game to him?"

"Who knows?" Luke threw up his hands.

"Yeah, let's get back to the station and let these guys do their job." Charlie tapped one of the officers on the shoulder. "Get a piece of that poster with the stain. I'm pretty sure I know what it is, but we've got to make sure."

"Good as done."

♣

"Well, Scottie the Hottie," Charlie paused, "That's what the ladies call you, right?"

Scottie glared at him, then flipped his eyes to a corner of the room.

Luke laughed as he tag-teamed with his brother-in-law. "Ah, Charlie, the ladies don't call him that. That's what he calls himself."

Scottie's nostrils flared and he gritted his teeth.

"Now there is no need for that. Just ask relevant questions," instructed Scottie's attorney who had appeared at the police station while they had been searching his client's apartment.

Charlie leaned toward the attorney. "And what was your name?"

The attorney, irritated at how quickly he'd been forgotten, replied firmly, "Mr. Andrew Greyson."

"All of my questions are relevant," growled Charlie.

The attorney's chair made scraping sounds as he slid back, in a vain attempt to distance himself from Charlie.

"So tell me, Scottie, why do you have that nickname?"

The attorney whispered in Scottie's ear.

Scottie inhaled deeply. Smugness replaced the anger on his handsome face. He relaxed and answered, "Why? You need some tips on how to turn on that pretty little minx you brought to town? You wanna keep her satisfied so she'll stay away from me?"

Charlie grinned and remained unruffled as he clenched his fists underneath the table. "So you think you're that good, huh?"

"Well," Scottie hunched his shoulders and nodded.

"So, why did your wife leave you if you're such a phenomenon in bed? Or is it just the young and inexperienced, and the old and desperate who find you irresistible?" Charlie heard the attorney stifle a laugh as Scottie's leer wilted. He cleared his throat, finished with the pissing contest. "You know we found your Darla Jean room. So tell us about that."

"I like taking pictures of pretty women."

"Darla Jean was the only woman in all of the pictures. You've got to do better than that. You were stalking her."

Scottie squirmed. "Look, you have it all wrong."

"Oh, really? You have a room covered with photos of her, all of which appear to have been taken without her knowledge, and objects that probably once belonged to her. Plus, you always seemed to be around when she needed a ride. So just how do I have it all wrong?" Charlie looked at Luke. "What does it sound like to you?"

"Yep, sounds like stalking to me. What about you, Mr. Attorney?" Luke shoved the pictures toward him.

"The name is Andrew Greyson," he reiterated as he looked at the photographs.

"Okay, so I have an obsession, but I never harmed her. Ever!" Scottie licked his dry lips. "It's like this, you see. I taught literature. I have a masters in romantic literature."

"Of course you do," Charlie agreed with an eye roll.

"No, I'm serious." Dark stains crept from Scottie's armpits. "I've read about women of near perfection and Darla Jean was that." He grabbed a fist of his dark unruly hair. Resting his elbows on the table, Scottie stared into space as he remembered her. "She was Venus, Godiva, Helen of Troy, and Mother Teresa all rolled into one. The essence of perfection." Scottie gazed at Charlie. "She was to be adored, worshiped, and treasured." He sighed, "Darla Jean was a goddess."

Charlie thought *this guy is warped beyond reason.* "So when your goddess was knocked off of her pedestal by becoming pregnant, you snapped."

Scottie swallowed hard. His mouth twisted and his eyes dulled.

"Is that why you killed her? She wasn't the saint you thought she was. Darla Jean was tainted and you couldn't stand it. Isn't that right, Scottie? She humiliated you. Toyed with you. The woman you worshiped was nothing but a bewitching slag."

Scottie's breath became ragged and deep. Baring his perfect teeth, he slammed his fists on the table. "Yes! She was a slut! A fraud! Darla Jean teased and taunted me with her flirtations. Stroking my arms, kissing my cheek, sending me Valentine's cards. Then when I tried to step up our relationship, she went all holy on me. Telling me she was a virgin and going to be a nun. That made her even more desirable. She was hot and sexy, yet pure and virtuous. So unattainable, like a dream." A pathetic smile limped across his full lips. "An angel."

Scottie began to scratch his head, trying to get her memories out of his brain. He stopped abruptly and looked at each man in the room. Pointing his finger at Charlie, he snarled, "She was a filthy liar. A demon sent to torment me." He sneered, "She told me that night she was pregnant. Described it as an immaculate conception."

He grunted. "She must have thought I was so enchanted by her, I'd believe her preposterous tale. So, yes, I wanted to rip off her pretty little lying head and parade it around town. To show the town that Miss Snow White was nothing but a lying whore. She made a fool out of me. She used me. Used me!" Scottie slammed his palm against his chest. "I don't like being used." He used his shirt sleeve to wipe the spit from his chin.

The attorney sputtered as he tried to make his client shut up. Scottie shrugged him away. He groaned as his head lolled around, "But I didn't. I didn't kill her."

"I need a few minutes with my client. Alone."

Charlie and Luke stood. "Take all the time you need." With his hand on the doorknob, Charlie turned and asked, "Why the rosary beads? Why shove them in her mouth?"

"Don't say anything, Scottie. Not another word comes out of your mouth! Do you understand?" Greyson wanted to try to salvage his case.

Charlie smirked as he stared at Scottie's dead look and thought, *not so hottie*.

Through the two-way glass, Charlie watched Scottie softly bang his forehead against the table as Greyson tried to calm him.

"Well, what do you think?" Luke asked as he watched the spectacle.

"The guy's a loon," replied Charlie.

Sergeant Mike Purvis slipped into the observation room holding two cups of coffee. Charlie accepted a cup from Mike. Luke waved away the other one. "I think he's a nut," Mike smirked, sipping the coffee.

"Yep," Charlie chuckled. "We should let him stew for a while. I want to talk to Matt Hoffsteader and Father Eli again."

Luke rubbed his chin. "Yeah, I agree, Mike, let ol' Scottie sweat for a few more minutes, then put him back into his cell." He slapped Charlie on the back. "Well, let's hit the road."

Chapter 17

"*The Steakhouse* said Matt's father called in sick for him," Luke reported as he hung up the phone in his office and started out.

"To his house, we go," Charlie said, as he fell in step with Luke.

Luke pulled onto Main Street. "You still think Matt and Father Eli are involved, even after what we've seen and heard from Scottie?"

Charlie tilted his head side-to-side. "Luke, never rule out anyone until you have all the facts. When we first questioned Matt, we didn't know about Darla Jean's pregnancy."

"Yeah, but he said he wanted to marry her. So what if she was pregnant?"

"That's the point. Matt *said* he wanted to marry her. But remember Jason said that Matt wasn't upset because he knew Darla Jean was determined to become a nun?"

"Right. So he might have made the whole thing up to make himself sound innocent. Yeah, I see. His father had plenty of time to coach him. Jason called right after he reported Darla Jean missing."

Charlie tapped his temple. "Yep. You have to remember the little things and think the worst of your suspects. And also, make note of the reactions of everyone in the room. At the time it may not seem like much, but later when you have more clues, those little gasps, widening of the eyes, and flinches make sense."

"What did you see that I didn't?"

"When Matt said that he wanted to marry Darla Jean, his mother looked at him with an odd expression. At the time, I didn't think too much about it but now … yeah, now I think it's because Matt never mentioned wanting to marry Darla Jean."

"We're almost there. We'll soon find out."

Ruth Hoffsteader opened the door. Before they could ask for Matt, she blurted, "Matthew is with David at his office." She flashed a business card. "My husband said to call him if you have any more questions. And for me not to speak to you. I'm sorry." Ruth slowly shut the door.

Charlie and Luke stared at the bright red door. "Well, I guess we'll just have to call David and have him bring Matt to the station."

Luke scratched his chin. "Yeah, makes me wonder if we have the wrong person in lockup."

"Hmm, after we talk to Father Eli again, we may think they all had a hand in Darla Jean's demise."

Luke unlocked the car door. "Yeah, like *Murder on The Orient Express*."

"I wouldn't laugh. Strange things happen all the time. Trust me. Let's go talk with Father Eli one more time." Charlie watched the town of Mercy slip by as Luke made his way to the church. "On second thought, let's go back to the station. Ma may still be with Father Eli discussing the wedding."

"Good. I'd rather question Matt than Father Eli."

♣

Two hours later, Matt Hoffsteader strolled into the station with his father. Charlie wondered if the two thought the tailor-made suits they were wearing would sway his opinion. Nope. He couldn't care less. Only words and body language mattered to him.

"Mr. Hoffsteader. Matt." Charlie greeted them with a firm handshake. "This way."

Luke was waiting for them in the interview room.

David Hoffsteader stated, "I'd like to make this quick. I have appointments. Matthew is innocent of any wrongdoing, but he is willing to answer any and all questions that may help apprehend Darla Jean Rogers' murderer."

Charlie mulled over David's declaration. He tapped the table three times with the tip of his pen. "I appreciate your cooperation. First question then. Matt, are you the father of Darla Jean's baby?" He was impressed with Mr. Hoffsteader's restraint, but there it was, the minuscule widening of his eyes. Either David Hoffsteader didn't know or maybe there was something else behind his eyes. Regardless, Matt knew Darla Jean was pregnant, but he had no reaction. *Stupid, stupid boy.*

Mr. Hoffsteader whispered in his son's ear. Matt hunched his shoulders.

"Is your client going to answer the question? Yes? No? Maybe? It's a pretty straightforward question."

"I don't know. She said I was." Matt slouched with a deadpan face.

Charlie leaned forward and glared at the arrogant boy. "You didn't want to be responsible for a baby. Is that why you killed her?"

David Hoffsteader interjected. "He admitted earlier he wanted to marry her. What difference would it make if she was pregnant?"

"Did you?"

Matt mimicked Charlie's posture. "Yeah, I said that."

Charlie smiled. *This boy is cagey, but not smart.* "Yes, I'm aware you *said* you wanted to marry her. But did you *want* to? There's a difference." He looked at Mr. Hoffsteader. "Surely, you can explain the subtle variance to your client."

While scrutinizing the ceiling's corner, Matt slid his tongue around his teeth and wished he could ignore the cops. But dear ol' Dad had made it clear he was to tell the truth or *see you later trust fund.*

Luke interrupted Matt's examination of his teeth. "Answer Detective McClung's question, now. For Pete's sake, I'd like to get home before midnight."

"Matthew, answer the question now. Let's get this over with pronto. I have people to see," instructed his father.

Matt dropped his eyes and glared at his father, then at the two detectives. They wanted the truth? He'd give them the ugly truth. Matt replied slowly, "No, I did not want to marry Darla Jean Rogers."

Charlie sighed, "Let me get this straight. You knew Darla Jean was pregnant and you didn't want to marry her?"

"Yep."

"Why not? I thought you loved her," asked Charlie.

Matt leaned against the table dangling his arms between his legs and sneered. "You see, it's like this. As long as I've known her, she always claimed she wanted to be a nun. A goody two-shoes up until she got back from college." Slouching back, he continued with a wicked grin, "She approached me saying she had a proposition. Free and easy sex with no strings attached." Matt scoffed, "Who would turn down a sweet piece like that? You know what I'm saying?"

David Hoffsteader coughed. "Matthew, please have some decorum."

Charlie was perplexed. "Did she explain why?"

"Yeah, said she wanted to experience life so she'd be able to counsel her students. Pff, whatever eased her conscience."

"So you didn't love her?"

"Look, like I said, she had droned on about the nun business for as long as I can remember, and there would never be me in her future. She made that perfectly clear. She was fun to hang with. I mean she was just one of the guys. Even paid her own way."

David Hoffsteader glanced at his watch. "Look, it appears that my son is not involved with Darla Jean's death, so I say we're done here." He stood, motioning his son to follow.

"Now, wait a minute. I do have a few more questions. I need to completely understand the dynamics of this strange and perverted relationship." Charlie stepped in front of the door. "Please sit back down."

He paced around the room massaging his earlobe. "So I understand you liked Darla Jean a lot, but you weren't necessarily in love with her, right?"

"Yeah." Matt sat up straight in his chair. Charlie's pacing made him nervous.

"And when she asked you to engage in a sexual relationship, you didn't hesitate? You literally jumped into bed with her?"

"Uhuh." Matt felt lines of sweat trailing down his back.

"Of course you did. Did you think you were the only one having sex with her? I mean, like you said, who wouldn't want to have sex with her." Charlie grabbed the edge of the table and leaned forward. "But that wouldn't have mattered since you didn't love her."

"Uhuh."

Charlie sat down and crossed his arms over his chest. "But what I don't understand is … is why you went back to her house to talk with her. I mean you followed her to the church and tried to talk with her. About what? What was so important that it couldn't wait? You had to talk with her right then. Can you explain that to me?"

Matt's mouth gaped like a fish out of water, "Well, uh, uh …"

Charlie answered, "Let me tell you what I think happened. I think you told her to get an abortion and she refused. You began to panic. What if her parents found out? They might force you to marry her. Then you'd be stuck with a girl you didn't love and a baby you wanted dead. So you killed two birds with one stone."

"No, it wasn't like that. I mean …"

"Stop this right now." David Hoffsteader yanked his son's arm. "Don't say another word." He scowled at Charlie. "Are you arresting my son?"

"No, not yet." Charlie stood in front of the door and held the doorknob.

"Come on, son, it's time to go," David ordered.

Charlie kept the door closed. "But before you go, we do need to draw some blood from your son. You know, to prove he is the father of the dead baby." Charlie thought *if looks could kill*, and grinned.

Luke flashed the court order. "Follow me."

Chapter 18

"Thanks for the pie and coffee, Thelma." Marian took a bite of cherry pie with vanilla ice cream.

Thelma swallowed some of the best coffee in town. "You paid for it. Remember the twenty?"

From the booth they shared, Marian looked around the diner and sighed. "This place is marvelous. I wish Lyman County had a place like this. Everything there has been modernized."

"Yep, this place has been around since 1939 and the only thing that's changed is brown leather upholstery to blue vinyl in 1960." Thelma ran her hand across a tear in the cushion caused from too many bottoms sliding across. "I think it's about time for another upholstery job."

"Have you lived here all your life?"

Thelma nodded as she slid a forkful of peach cobbler into her mouth.

"I bet you can tell me the history of the McClung clan."

"That I can. But I'm thinking you want to know more about Charlie." Thelma pointed her fork at Marian then dove for more cobbler.

"So, tell me all you know about Charlie, please."

"Every girl in town was in love with him. I even heard tell that Josephine had a crush on him. But I wouldn't worry about it. That old cow gets heated up by any good-looking male. That man of yours loves you with all of his being. I can see that by the way he lights up when your name's mentioned. Yep, Charlie is a good, honest man and devoted to his family."

Marian giggled. "He sounds too good to be true."

"What can I say? You've got yourself a fine man. Your own knight in shining armor."

"What about the rest of the family?"

Thelma scraped the remaining cobbler into a neat pile in the center of the plate. Picking up her coffee mug, she winked at Marian. "Well, you're going to be bored because there's not much to tell. The whole McClung clan is the most caring and law-abiding bunch of people I've ever known. Yeah, there are some quirky characters, like Aunt Ella. Never goes anywhere without a hat."

Thelma leaned in and whispered, "And another thing, just between us because no one around here speaks about it, but Granny McClung could read people.

"What do you mean read people?"

"Granny McClung would touch someone and she'd get *feelings.*"

Marian's brows drew together. "Feelings?"

"Like if someone was going to get sick." She saw Marian wince. "Oh, she didn't predict anyone's death. Nothing like that. I personally think she had overly sensitive hands and could feel a fever before the fever had set in." Thelma scooped the remaining cobbler into her mouth and washed it down with coffee. "Although, she had a knack for knowing who was right for you." She set down the mug. "Now that was pretty eerie. Nine times out of ten, she got it right."

Marian asked, "You mean a soul mate. How could she tell by just touching them?" She grinned, "How do you know this?"

Thelma held up her empty mug and tapped it with a long blood-red fingernail to get the waitress's attention. The waitress scurried over and filled the empty mug and warmed up Marian's.

"My mother. She and Granny McClung were best friends." Thelma blew on the steaming coffee.

"So how do you know she got it right most of the time?"

Thelma rested her forearms on the table. "My mother said when Granny McClung shook a couple's hands and said, 'It *was* a pleasure to meet you,' after a few weeks or months, they'd no longer be a couple. But if she said, 'It's so nice to meet you two,' then they'd be together forever. Well, until one of them died that is."

"Hmmm, anyone else in the family have that gift?"

"Nope, I think it died with Granny McClung." Thelma shook her head. "I should have never told you that. I'm sorry. Really, they are good people. You couldn't be marrying into a better family. And you're all they've been talking about since they found out about you. Hell, the whole town's been waiting to meet you."

Marian smiled. "I guess that means they're well thought of in the community."

"To say the least." Thelma waved her hands in the air. "Let's move on to another subject. Murder. We haven't had one since I don't know when."

Marian shivered. "I hope they catch whoever did it soon."

"Charlie and Luke arrested one of our cab drivers. Looks pretty bad for him. Theodore found a picture of the dead girl sticking out of his locker."

"Scottie the Hottie?"

Thelma laughed, "So, you've already heard of him? There've been hushed rumors about him and the dead girl."

Marian ate the last bite of her pie. "Do a lot of girls think Scottie is a hottie?"

Thelma raised her eyebrows. "Now this is all gossip, no facts you understand, but the word is lonely older women, like Dora, one of the waitresses at Higgins, and Josephine, to name a couple sure thought so. And there's the occasional frustrated wife, plus all the young naïve girls."

The man likes to prey on the desperate and inexperienced it seems, Marian thought. "Are there any other suspects?"

"Hell, yeah, Father Eli and that boyfriend of hers, Matt."

"What?" Marian gasped. "I can't believe Father Eli would be involved in anything hideous like that."

"Gossip and rumors that's all it is. What else does a tiny town like this have to do but talk and speculate? Don't worry your pretty head about any of it. Besides, now they've got your wedding to talk about."

Thelma was right. She and Charlie were to be married in three days. Marian figured Thelma being in the taxi business, probably had her finger on the pulse of the town. And she wanted this murder over and done with. "Thelma, why would anyone want to kill that girl? I mean, I heard she was about to join the convent."

Thelma smoothed a graying mass of black hair away from her face. "To be honest with you, I don't know. Some people are saying that Matt Hoffsteader, her boyfriend, was jealous of Scottie and flew into a jealous rage and killed her. And some are saying the same about Scottie."

She ran her long skinny finger around the empty dessert plate hoping to collect any remaining residue from the cobbler. Thelma sighed. "I know I shouldn't, but I'm getting more cobbler. More pie for you?"

Marian shook her head. "I'm getting married Sunday. But you go ahead. I want to know why people think Father Eli had anything do with the girl's death."

"Ah, just rumors. Nothing to them."

"Tell me. It may help solve the case."

Thelma ordered more cobbler while the waitress refilled their mugs. "Well, some think it's too big of a coincidence that she was found in his armoire. I mean, she had to be killed at the church."

"But what reason would he have to kill her?"

Thelma mouthed, "Blackmail."

Marian considered the idea. Father Eli was very attractive and young. Maybe he fell into temptation. Maybe the dead girl wasn't such a good girl after all. "She wasn't pregnant was she?"

Thelma shrugged. "I did hear that rumor just today." The waitress set a heaping plate of peach cobbler before her.

Marian popped her knuckles. "So three suspects with probable cause. What about her parents or his? Did any of them have a problem with her?"

Thelma looked at Marian. "Hon, leave the crime solving to your intended and your future brother-in-law. I really don't mean to be rude. But I hear all kinds of trash every day." She smiled like the Cheshire cat. "What I want to talk about is your wedding? Tell me all about it."

Chapter 19

There was a soft echo in the church as Charlie and Luke walked to Father Eli's office. Charlie knew they would be closer to his office if they came through the side door, but he always entered from the front. He found the stained glass, the glow of the candles, and the faint scent of incense that clung to the air familiar and comforting. His mind murmured a prayer for Granny and Pop. It made him happy to know they were together in heaven, but sad that they would not witness him marry the one they had been waiting for. Charlie glanced upward. Maybe they would.

Father Eli's door was open. He was unhooking the last heavy curtain, snuffing out the sunlight. Charlie was curious why he wanted the curtains closed. The light filtering through the windows was uplifting. "Good afternoon, Father," Charlie greeted.

Father Eli wore a look of feigned happiness. "Come in, have a seat," he welcomed them as he settled behind his desk. "Would you like coffee, tea?"

"No, hopefully, this won't take long." Charlie tried to relax. He hated having to interview Father Eli, but he had a job to do and it had to be done. "I wish we were here to talk about the wedding. And by the way, thank you for that."

Father Eli nodded.

"Anyway, I'll get straight to the point." Charlie rested his forearms on his thighs. "Did you give Darla Jean a set of red rosary beads?"

"Yes, they belonged to me."

"Was there any significance to the rosary beads? I mean, why did you give her your personal beads?"

"I gave them to her because she wanted mine for some reason. If I had to guess, maybe she wanted something to remind her of her home church."

"I see." Charlie shifted. "Did she always pray in the sanctuary after confession?"

"Yes, but occasionally she'd use the prayer closet."

"So are you positive she was praying in the sanctuary when you left her that night?" Charlie's gaze returned to the closed curtains.

Father Eli started to speak then paused for a few seconds. "I can't honestly say she was. I left her standing in the sanctuary, but I didn't actually see Darla Jean kneel in prayer."

Charlie stood. "Can we see the prayer closet?"

Father Eli led them to the small, windowless room. A rather plain floor lamp stood in one corner. A small table with two tiers of unlit candles, one row white, the other red, stood in the opposite corner. The glow from a semi-circle of candles caressed the simple crucifix standing before the well-worn kneeler. An intricate tapestry rug covered the floor. A well-padded bench and small side table completed the furnishings.

Charlie entered the solemn room. He picked up a thick Bible and saw a set of rosary beads. Picking up the beads, he held them under the floor lamp. "Did your rosary beads look like these?"

"Yes, but mine were glass, those are plastic. Josephine always keeps a set of red rosary beads in here. In case someone forgets to bring their own."

Charlie watched the light reflect off the shiny plastic beads. "Why red?'

"To remind people that our Savior shed His blood for them."

He returned the beads. "They look like the ones that were stuffed in Darla Jean's mouth."

Father Eli gasped, "In her mouth?"

"Yes, let's go back to your office. You said Darla Jean would occasionally use this room. Was there any reason she chose one over the other?"

Father Eli led the way. "I can't honestly answer that question. As you saw, the prayer closet is hidden away for privacy. The only reason I know she used it is I would see her coming up the hallway when I passed by the end there." He pointed to the next turn in the hallway which passed Josephine's suite and then led to his office.

Charlie and Luke stopped just outside Father Eli's office. "Can you run through that night from the first time you saw Darla Jean to the last?"

Father Eli walked into his office and leaned back on the front of his desk and began. "I was in the sanctuary praying. She walked in and asked to make a confession." He shook his head. "I don't know the time but it was late."

"When do you lock the doors?" Charlie asked.

Luke answered, "Only the side doors are locked after the six o'clock mass."

"That's right and Josephine locks all the rooms except the prayer closet. I unlock them at four in the morning. But I digress." Father Eli gave a little jump and sat on top of his desk. "Her confession was as usual ..." he exhaled. " But she did say something that I thought nothing of at the time. Now I understand what she meant."

Father Eli snapped his fingers as he tried to remember Darla Jean's exact words. "She said, 'Bless the new life within me.' Yes, those were her words. I thought she meant the Holy Spirit, or being forgiven, and starting with a clean slate for the next day." He stared at Charlie and Luke. "I mean, why would I think otherwise?"

"Well, you knew she was having sex," Luke reminded him.

Father Eli pulled his head back. "I ... well ... I guess I've always thought of her as a good girl. A little flawed, but a good girl."

Charlie tugged his earlobe. It was about time the good priest realized the truth. "She was seeing Matt and Scottie." He shrugged. "We're sure she was having sex with Matt, but not so sure about Scottie. Just finish telling us about that night."

Clearing his throat, Father Eli continued, "She said she wanted to pray. The last time I saw her she was standing in front of the prayer candles, the ones to the right of the altar. I returned to my office to check my calendar for the next day and take care of a few things. Then I went to Josephine's room and asked her to go to the sanctuary and check on Darla Jean in about fifteen minutes. I then retired to my bedroom to finish my prayers." He held up his open palms. "That's the last time I saw her alive."

"And you didn't see anyone else in the sanctuary?"

"No."

Charlie scratched his head. "Got any questions, Luke?"

"Yeah. Did Josephine tell you she had checked on Darla Jean and she was gone?"

"No. But there is no reason why Josephine would tell me that."

Luke puckered his lips. "When did the men arrive to pick up the armoire?"

Father Eli shook his head. "I don't know. Josephine handles things like that."

Charlie stood and reached for Father Eli's hand. "Thank you for your time. Marian and I will be seeing you soon."

Father Eli beamed. He was looking forward to the joyous occasion. Tomorrow, he would be saying his last goodbyes to Darla Jean.

"Father, I have two more things. Do you have the number for the moving company?"

He nodded as he flipped through a huge Rolodex. "Sure thing. Josephine is very efficient, duplicates all of her records for me." Father Eli pulled out a card giving it to Charlie. "This is the place. And what is the other thing you need?"

Charlie scratched his cheek. "Yeah, I hate to ask you this but we need to get some blood. Just for procedural sake, to rule you out as the father of Darla Jean's baby."

He inhaled deeply and exhaled, "Where do I go for the blood work?"

Charlie didn't want to humiliate the priest by having him come to the station. "I'll have Dylan or Mary Grace stop by."

"I appreciate your thoughtfulness, Charlie."

♣

Luke and Charlie walked into the office of the moving company. There were only two in town. This one had only been in Mercy City for a little over a year.

"I'm Detective McClung and this is Detective O'Sullivan. We're with the Mercy City police and are here to speak to someone about the armoire that was picked up from Saint Fergus Catholic Church and delivered to *The Antique Shop* on Main Street."

The middle-aged woman shivered. "The one with the dead girl. Just a minute, the guys are in the back."

Charlie gazed out the store front. "Do you know these people well?"

"Yeah, well enough. Their kids play ball with our Ben and James."

"Then you can ask the questions."

Four hefty men greeted them. The oldest one spoke, "Hi, Luke, I understand you've got some questions about the armoire delivery."

Luke introduced Charlie to the men. "Ethan, did you pick up the armoire?"

The owner of the company answered, "That I did. Me and my oldest boy there," Ethan pointed to the shortest of the four tall men.

"Did you notice anything unusual about the delivery?"

The older man rubbed his shoulder. "Well, they had it all tied up and wrapped. We didn't have to do anything but pick it up, load it into the truck and unload it at your wife's shop."

"Did you ask them to do that? I mean tie it and wrap it."

"No, I just figured they wanted to know the thing was properly protected. So they did it themselves."

"Was it heavier than you thought it would be, or make any strange noises?"

"Nah, I mean it was heavy, but you'd expect that from the size of the thing. It made a sound like something shifting inside. I just thought it was the shelves knocking around."

"So, you never looked inside of it?"

"Nope. We just picked it up and dropped it off. Had your wife Rachel sign for it and then we were history."

Luke bounced his pen against his notepad. "Did you see anyone at the church?"

Ethan responded. "The side door was unlocked just like the lady said it would be, and it was sitting where she said it would be. Didn't see nobody the whole time we were there. Just left the paperwork on the table there in the foyer like she said to."

"Was the lady's name Josephine Mendel?"

"Yeah, I believe that was her name. Say, hon, wasn't that the lady you spoke to?" Ethan asked the woman who had greeted them.

"Yes, dear, that was her name all right," she replied.

Luke continued, "What time did you pick up the armoire and then deliver it to *The Antique Shop*?"

"It was Wednesday, around eight in the morning. We had a few more pickups and deliveries after that. It was probably, I'd say, around two when we finally dropped it at the store."

Luke huffed with frustration and looked to Charlie. "Detective McClung, do you have any questions?"

"Did any of you know Darla Jean Rogers on a first-name basis?"

They all nodded. Ethan answered for them, "We all did. She waitressed at *The Steakhouse*. Real friendly."

Charlie walked closer to the group and addressed the son. "Tell me your name, again?"

"Joey."

"Can you hold out your hands? I guess in this business you get a lot of those," commented Charlie about his many bruises and cuts.

"Yes, sir, we all do." The other three men held out their arms to confirm Joey's statement.

Charlie bobbed his head and asked, "Did you ever go out with her?"

"Naw, not my type. She was pretty and all that, but I like girls with more meat on their bones." Joey blushed.

Charlie grinned as he looked at the boy who could be an NFL linebacker. "I understand, son. I think that's all for me."

"Well, if you remember anything, give me a call." Luke handed him a business card.

Charlie paused in the doorway and drummed his fingers on the frame, "I understand you did this job for free?"

"Yeah, I like helping out the church." Ethan shrugged shyly. "I figured no good deed goes unnoticed."

"You're a wise man." Charlie stepped through the doorway to leave. He paused and looked at Ethan thinking he was in bad need of a haircut, then he whispered something to Luke.

Luke jerked his head toward Ethan who was teasing the receptionist. He made a quick scribble on his notepad, *Ethan - graying brown hair.*

Chapter 20

"NO! GET OUT OF HERE! NOW!" Sarah shoved Charlie out of the family room. Emma, Rachel, and Sophia stood behind her challenging him to enter.

"What the …?" Charlie stumbled over Luke as his sister-in-law dared them to move forward.

Ma, hidden from sight, bellowed, "Ya can't come in, son. Marian is indecent."

Charlie leered at the women. "Sounds like an invitation to me."

Backing away from the opposition, Luke answered, "Nope, I know the fury of the McClung women. Even the devil would run." He turned and yelled, "Da! Where are you?"

"In here son, come away from the lot of them harpies."

Luke headed to the aromatic kitchen.

"And you call yourself a copper," teased Charlie. "Now, let me have a peek at Marian." He moved forward playfully but froze as Ma stepped around the women. "Uh, yes, all right now … uh, I'll be joining Da in the kitchen." Raucous laughter chased him as he fled the scene of his near assault.

"And ya best be stayin' in there." Ma returned to Marian, now dressed. "Aw, ya look like a blessed angel. That ya do."

Sarah wiped away a tear and sighed, "Oh, Marian, you are an answer to prayer." She wrapped her arms around Marian. "Charlie has waited so long for you. So very long." Sarah held her at arm's length. "Thank you for loving him, for loving us."

"Here you go." Emma and Rachel set down a full-length mirror they had carried from granny's bedroom. Both gasped, stunned by Marian's beauty. Emma spoke first, "None of us could pull off wearing Ma's wedding dress. But you ... I'm utterly gobsmacked!"

Marian stepped in front of the mirror. She touched her cheek and then the mirror. She wondered what Lee would think as she remembered their wedding day. A simple white gown and veil. The memory disappeared with the sound of Lee's voice, *open a new book*.

She ran her trembling hands down the bodice. The dress fit perfectly around her petite waist and the flutter sleeves accentuated her firm shoulders. The plunging neckline stopped to show a modest amount of cleavage. She turned to see the train. The Irish lace floated down and puddled on the floor. "Oh, Ma," choked Marian. She wiped away a single tear. "This is so beautiful. I can't ..."

Ma embraced her as the tears flowed freely. "Ah, child, why are ya cryin'?"

"I'm so happy. It's been so very long since I've been truly happy." Marian inhaled Ma's sweet scent and absorbed the love she offered. She felt at peace.

"Here," Ma offered her a tissue, "wipe ya face. We're not finished just yet." She turned and scanned the room. "Sophia, bring ya grandma that flat box."

Sophia held the box while Ma delicately removed its contents. Now my pet, turn and look in the mirror while I put this on ya."

Marian obeyed. Her eyes beheld the treasure as Ma placed the veil on her head. A dainty silver crown encrusted with pearls and diamonds held a sheer lace panel that draped down and around her hips.

"What'd ya girls think about ya sister-to-be?"

"She's beautiful," murmured Sarah.

Emma and Rachel sighed, "Breathtaking."

Sophia wrapped her arms around Marian's waist. "You're a princess if I ever did see one."

Ma walked around Marian looking her up and down. "We need to get ya bejeweled. I know just the right earrings and necklace for ya." She noticed the crinkle in Marian's brow. "Don't ya worry. Gonna keep it simple. Just some pearls will do ya."

"I feel so guilty. You're doing so much for me."

Ma smacked her bottom. "Ya stop that kinda talkin'. Ya my daughter, now." She looked at her daughters. "Tell her now. Am I doing more for her than I did for you?"

There was a collective no. Rachel added, "You should be happy that Ma only has three days to fuss over you. Believe me."

Sarah clapped, "Okay, I've a list of things that you have to decide. There's flowers, food, music, and bridesmaids."

"Well, of course, all of you will be in the wedding. You decide who'll be matron of honor and you can pick out your own dresses. I only request the color be in the purple family."

"I'll be matron of honor since I'm the oldest," declared Sarah. "How many do you want, Marian?"

"I'm easy. Whatever you decide is fine." Marian smiled to hide her second thoughts and began to pop her knuckles. *Joan's going to kill me, but there's no way she can drop everything without more notice. Maybe I should call her. Things are happening so fast. Maybe having a second ceremony at Primrose will soothe her fury. Maybe—* her thoughts were interrupted.

"Four! Sarah, Mary Grace, Rachel, and me," declared Emma. "Because you know, Charlie will have Sean, Dylan, Luke, and Mike Purvis as his groomsmen. Gotta keep it even."

"Oh, please let me and my brother Ryan play the music. Pleaseee?" begged Sophia.

Ma quickly agreed, "They make such a heavenly sound, Marian. Ya can't go wrong with a violin and a harp."

"Sounds good and you can pick the music. I trust you." Marian laughed as Sophia gave her a bear hug. "That leaves food and flowers."

Ma voiced her opinion, "If ya ask me since it'll be near one o'clock by the time it's all done, I think it should be a full meal. What'd ya think?"

Marian twisted her mouth in thought, "Yeah, but can a caterer do it on such a short notice? We don't even know how many people will attend."

"Pssh! That's nothing. I gotta army of ladies to help. The whole town will be there. We'll be havin' the traditional foods, soda bread with cheese, potato and leek soup for starters." Ma's fingers drummed on her chin as she thought. "And for the main course, we'll be havin' beef stew for sure. Fish, we've gotta have fish but salmon? I don't know—"

Marian clasped Ma's hands. "Ma, if it's the cost, don't worry about that. I will pay for everything."

"Don't ya say a thing like that! You're our daughter."

The sound of "our daughter" sent a rush of warmth to Marian's heart. She hugged Ma tightly. "Thank you for making me feel loved, wanted, and a part of you." She settled her hands on Ma's shoulders. "But I am paying for this wedding. It is not up for debate. So salmon it is! I want a traditional Irish wedding feast." Marian kissed her new mother's cheek. "I love you, Ma." She held out her hand beckoning the other women to join for a group hug. "I love you all."

Ma pursed her full lips and consented, knowing she had met her match. "All right then, now. A traditional Irish feast ya will have. So let's start over, soda bread and cheeses with potato and leek soup for starters. The main course we'll be havin' melon and avocado salad, beef stew, potato rolls, salmon with colcannon, and orange-glazed carrots. For dessert, there'll be the weddin' cake, of course, and chocolate-dipped strawberries. Can't be without the whiskey-soaked fruit cake." Cupping Marian's chin, Ma asked, "Are ya happy now, my pet?"

"Yes, but what to drink?"

Sarah gave a hearty laugh. "Drink you ask? What won't there be to drink? Right Emma, Rach?"

Emma shook her head. "Yeah, don't worry Da will make sure no one goes thirsty."

"Hmm, that takes care of the food, music, drink, and the wedding party. That just leaves the flowers," Sarah rattled off the to-do list. "Oh, and the cake, the decoration of the cake?"

Marian grinned, "A simple bouquet of lavender and baby's breath."

"Aye, I have that in the garden. It's good as done." Ma clapped her hands. "Oh, my Marian, ya Aunt Ella will be wantin' ta make the cake. She's a fine baker, that she is." Ma looked at the dainty watch on her wrist. "She'll be here any second now."

Sophia pretended to faint on the couch. "When you eat one of her cakes, you'll think you've died and gone to heaven."

Marian smiled, "I think we have a plan now for the execution of *Operation Wedding*."

♣

Charlie looked over Da's shoulder and inhaled the intoxicating rich aroma of his famous shepherd's pie that had just come out of the oven. "Da, you must have been a chef in another life."

Two empty beer bottles sat on the oversized island. Da reached into the refrigerator and pulled out three more. "Son, I think ya been wantin' this. Luke, drink up." Da downed half his bottle. "Ya Ma is drivin' me crazy with all of this weddin' talk." He finished the bottle and retrieved another one. "Tah, but I'm thankful I've got only 'til Sunday and it'll be done." Da winked at Charlie. "Aye, son, she's happy for ya, that she is."

Charlie tilted the bottle, letting the stout Irish beer rush down his throat. It had taken him a few years to appreciate its flavor. "I think I'll just stay out of their way and agree to whatever they want."

"Here's to that," Da clinked his bottle against Charlie's and Luke's. "Enough of weddin' talk. Luke tells me ya got more suspects than ya need."

"Yep, seems like Darla Jean wasn't the good girl after all." Charlie made himself comfortable at the kitchen island. "Once we think we've found the right one, another one pops into the picture."

"What's ya gut tellin' ya?"

Charlie turned to Luke. "Well, tell us what you think."

Luke scratched his forehead and finished his bottle. "That's a tricky one." He dug into the refrigerator for another beer. "At first I thought it was Matt until Scottie came into the picture. Then, you can't forget about Father Eli. He was the last person to see her alive." He rested his elbows on the oversized countertop. "Now there's Ethan. He knew her. He knew about the armoire. And he has graying brown hair."

Charlie massaged his earlobe. "Josephine has graying brown hair and the armoire is probably full of her hair. So ...," he shrugged. "I wouldn't put him on the top of the list. We need to start ruling out some of them." He tossed his empty bottle in the trash and accepted the one Da offered. "If I had to put them in order, I'd put Matt at the top, then Scottie, and I hate to say it, but Father Eli, and then Ethan."

Da picked up the shepherd's pie. "Follow me boys, we can continue this discussion while we ready the table for supper."

Charlie's stomach growled as he trailed after the alluring scent of the pie. He wanted to be with his family while they enjoyed their time with Marian. He didn't want to be chasing after perverts and murderers. But he smiled as he thought of his soon-to-be wife and the honeymoon.

Da disturbed his fantasy. "Well, what ya need to do is find out for sure where they all were at the time she was killed."

"Da, you know it's not that easy. People lie, and people lie for them." Charlie took a stack of plain white everyday china and placed one plate in front of each of the twenty chairs.

Luke shadowed him and placed the napkins and silverware. "I have Theodore checking Scottie's log book and fares. That's one we can verify."

Da returned from the kitchen with another shepherd's pie. "I got one more warming in the bottom oven. Luke, go fetch it and put it at the other end."

Charlie and Da stood with their arms crossed taking inventory of the table. Everything was ready to go except the baskets of fresh baked bread to sop up the sauce from the pie and, of course, the beer and wine.

"Wish me luck, son. I'm gonna fetch the women." Da hung his head and slowly made his way to the living room as the sounds of the clucking women grew louder.

As if on cue, the front door flew open and Aunt Ella, followed by the rest of the McClung clan, scrambled through the door like a swarm of army ants in pursuit of prey. "I smell Grandpa's shepherd's pie," yelled Mary Grace.

Da was relieved to see Ma leading her gang out of the living room to investigate the rampage through her house. He slid his arm around his happy wife and kissed her flushed cheek. "Supper's all ready for ya, love."

"Did ya make a salad like I asked ya to?"

He kissed her again. "In the fridge, now get yaself to ya chair. I'll fetch it."

♣

Charlie cradled Marian against his chest as they relaxed on his parents' front porch swing. The sounds of laughter and love filtering through the walls of the house and the warmth of Charlie's body made Marian feel safe. Brilliant specks of light began to dot the falling night. Cicadas, frogs, and katydids sang in harmony.

She sighed. "I love it here with you, just being." Marian said a silent prayer of thanks for the peace and comfort she found with Charlie and his family.

"Mmm, this is good." Charlie kissed the top of her head and squeezed her a little tighter. "I'm so glad we're getting married Sunday."

Marian sat up. The lights from the living room radiated around Charlie's head. *My angel,* she thought. "Really, it's not too quick?"

"Are you kidding me? I wish we had gotten married at the courthouse today." Charlie held her hands. "Now look me in the eyes. Is this what *you* want?" He held up one finger to stop her interruption.

"Wait. I know Ma is behind all of this. She never gave us a chance to talk about it. It's not too late to put her in reverse if this is not what you want. I mean it."

Without hesitation, Marian answered, "Yes, this is what I want. I want to be a part of your family's traditions." She wrapped her arms around him. "This is a totally new life for me. I've been stuck in limbo, not really living, just going through the motions." Leaning back, she studied his face. "I need different. I need this, Charlie. I need you, your family, and all the chaos that comes with it." She grinned and in her best Irish accent she said, "Ah, 'tis gonna be a grand weddin'."

Charlie kissed the tip of her nose. "All I want is for you to be happy."

Her shoulders sagged as she sighed.

"What's this for?" Charlie rubbed her fallen shoulders.

"Joan. I wish Joan could be here."

"Have you even asked her?"

Marian shook her head.

Charlie jumped up, pulling her with him. "Well now, let's just go give her a ring."

♣

Marian held the phone away from her ear. Taking a deep breath, she enunciated each word firmly, "Joan, please calm down, now!"

"Why should I? You've hurt me deeply. Do you understand that? I've been your only and truest friend since Lee died. And you run away to get married without me!"

"Now, be fair. This was not planned. It just happened. And I never said you weren't invited."

"Oh, like I'm to drop everything. You know I can't abandon the restaurant and forget about it like you've done me."

Marian felt anger welling up inside. "How dare you say that? I think it's poor management if you can't leave your restaurant for a few days without it falling to pieces."

Charlie forced the phone from Marian's hand. "Joan, this is Charlie … now … now calm down." He motioned for Marian to leave the room and mouthed, *go find Ma.*

She could hear Joan squawking, but left the room to find Ma in the kitchen.

Charlie let Joan fume until she ran out of breath. "Joan, you know Marian loves you. She's been worried sick about how you would handle this. How can you treat her this way when she's happier than she's been in years? And YET she's concerned about your feelings. This is supposed to be about her, not you. You're acting like a dried up, bitter old crow. Instead, why don't you act like the friend you claim to be?"

Joan began to cry. "I'm sorry. You're right. She's right," she sniffled.

"No, I'm sorry. I didn't mean to make you cry. But I love my Marian and I don't like seeing her upset." Charlie shifted his weight from foot to foot. "Look, I know she wants you here. Make her happy, Joan."

Joan blew her nose. "All right, I'll be there but ... can we make it a surprise?"

"Even better. I'll have one of my sisters call you. I know nothing. Just show up the day of and say I do. That's what I've been told."

Joan snorted a laugh. "Sounds good, Charlie. I need to speak with Marian and apologize for being such a bonehead."

Charlie found Marian and the McClung women gathered around the massive kitchen island eating scones and drinking hot tea. He picked up the cup sitting in front of Marian. Taking a sip, he grinned, "You know there's whiskey in this?"

She took the cup and sipped while batting her eyelashes at him. "So?"

"I didn't know I was marrying a lush." Charlie looked at Ma. "Can you make a cup for me? And Marian, Joan wants to finish your conversation. She's waiting on the phone."

Marian rushed out of the room.

"Tah, the poor thing is upset about her friend," Ma sighed.

Charlie tapped his finger on his lips and pretended to lock his lips. Then he pointed to each female. "All of you promise me you'll not be saying a word about what I've got to say, or none of you will hear my secret."

All swore to silence leaning toward him, eager to hear.

"I'm holding you to it. Only three days to keep your tongues to yourselves, okay?"

They all nodded in agreement.

"Good, Joan is going to surprise Marian. She'll be here on Sunday for the wedding. You all figure out whatever you women do in weddings and find her a place to stay. One of you will need to call Joan to coordinate the plan."

Sarah whispered, "I'll do it."

Marian returned with a sad smile. "We patched things up, but Joan said she's got a huge wedding happening this weekend and can't get away, but for us to take plenty of pictures."

"Oh, my goodness! Pictures! We forgot the photographer!" Sarah screamed. "I can't believe we forgot about a photographer!"

"Shush, child. Ya know Tom Linden can do it?"

Mary Grace giggled, "You'll like him. Tom thinks he's Rod Stewart."

Charlie poured another cup of tea. "Prances around enough, but he's a fine photographer." He splashed a few drops of whiskey in the strong brew. "The Braves must've won from the sound of it," Charlie said, responding to a boisterous cheer resounding from the living room.

Yawning, Marian apologized. "I don't mean to be rude, but I'm going to head upstairs to bed." She kissed everyone goodnight. Charlie slid his arm down her back and followed her up the stairs.

At the bedroom door, Charlie pulled her against his chest and leered. "In three days, I'll be able to go into that room with you."

"Really, our honeymoon will be in your parents' house?" She joked.

He nuzzled her ear. "Mmm, it'll make it that much more exciting."

"Aren't you afraid I'll shock your Ma with my screams and moans of ecstasy? There'll be ecstasy, right? I haven't waited this long for ho-hum," pouted Marian.

Tantalizingly surprised by her unexpected brazenness, he chuckled, "Well now, I guess it's a good thing I booked the whole *Rose Cottage Bed and Breakfast* this afternoon."

Marian gasped. "Ma pointed it out this morning. It's perfect for a honeymoon. But really? The whole house?"

He nodded. "Yep, the whole place. I don't want to share you with anyone."

She slid her hands up Charlie's chest to his neck, pulling his head toward hers. The gentle kiss grew more passionate as Marian ran her fingers through his hair. She broke the kiss and grinned wickedly. "Just a tiny sample of what's to come. Good night, Charlie." She slowly opened the door and disappeared.

Chapter 21

Charlie stared at the closed door. She had exposed a side she had kept well-hidden these past three months. Yeah, he certainly had found the one that granny had said was waiting for him. He had to get his mind off Marian. No way could he go to sleep after a kiss like that. Laughter floated up the stairway.

He passed Aunt Ella coming up the stairs. "Staying the night, again?"

"Aye, ya Ma trusts our Marian. It's ya she's worryin' 'bout if ya know wha' I mean." She winked and swatted his butt.

"That's why I'm joining them in the kitchen."

"Good on ya." Aunt Ella slipped into the bedroom where Marian was fast asleep.

Charlie hugged Ma. "So, you think you can pull off this wedding in three days?"

She threw his arm away from her shoulders. "Ya no son of mine if ya be questionin' my abilities to get ya married properly." Ma eased from the chair. "I gotta get me beauty sleep. Up at the crack of dawn in the mornin'. Now, get over here and kiss ya Ma goodnight."

Charlie planted a wet kiss on her forehead. "I love you, Ma. Thank you."

"Of course ya do."

Da and Ma saw the rest of the family to the front door. Only Dylan, Luke, and Sean stayed behind with Da rejoining them in the kitchen after seeing Ma to bed.

Dylan handed Da a mug of coffee as he settled into Ma's empty chair. "Let's get this murder solved before the weddin'. I don't want nothing interfering with ya day, son." Da rubbed his palms together, eager to be part of the police investigation, even if it was from the outside. "Let's throw out the facts."

"Well," Dylan started, "I got the paternity test results. Matthew Hoffsteader is the father of Darla Jean's baby."

Luke tapped his finger against his warm cup. "That puts him as the lead suspect. What do you think, Charlie?"

"Yeah, but let's get all the facts together first before we cut Scottie loose, that's if he hasn't already made bail. We're waiting for the film we found in Darla Jean's camera to be developed. Maybe it will put the last nail in his coffin. We'll have to wait and see." Charlie began to tick off the facts on his fingers. "We know she was strangled from behind."

Dylan nodded in confirmation.

"According to Father Eli, he last saw her around eleven-fifteen and Josephine said Darla Jean was gone by eleven-thirty. So she must have been killed between eleven-fifteen and one in the morning."

Sean interjected. "That's if you believe the two. Charlie, you know better than I do, you can't let your preconceived notions about their character get in the way."

"But until we get anything to disprove their statements, we'll have to accept them," defended Luke.

Charlie continued, "Darla Jean was not the good girl everyone thought she was. She was pregnant with Matt's baby. Now, it appears she was stringing Scottie along as well, and who knows who else Darla Jean was toying with, maybe even Father Eli, and don't forget about Ethan." He began to pace around the kitchen.

"I mean she could have been blackmailing Father Eli. Maybe that's why he was so eager to sell the armoire. Or Ethan, maybe? He knew about the armoire. An easy way to stash the body and put the blame on Father Eli." Charlie stared out the window into the blackness of the night. He was missing something. But what? If he could see that one thing that was teasing him just beyond his third eye.

Da cleared his throat, intruding on Charlie's contemplations. "Tell me her injuries and what kind of evidence was found at the scene."

"She was strangled with a curtain tieback, a red one. A set of red rosary beads were stuffed in her mouth after she was killed. There was bruising on her forearms and shins. Tests confirm the scratches on her neck were caused by her. She was not a virgin and had consensual sex the night she died. Plus, she was eight weeks pregnant with Matthew Hoffsteader's baby." Dylan puffed out his cheeks. "That about sums it up on injuries. Oh …," he snapped his fingers. "It appears an earring was torn from her right earlobe. A small gold loop was in the left one."

The men heard clopping on the steps and shuffling toward the kitchen. Marian stood in the archway wearing a pale pink terrycloth robe and fuzzy pink slippers. Her hair was a bit frazzled.

Charlie wondered what happened to the sexy, pink nightgown she had on in the morning, but still thought she was the most exquisite woman he'd ever known.

She hid a big yawn behind her hand. "Am I disrupting something?" Marian asked shyly. "It's just Aunt Ella's ... well, let's just say I can't fall back to sleep."

"Aye, the woman snores like a lumberjack that she does," Da grunted and patted the chair beside him. "Sit here child. Maybe ya can solve the puzzle we men can't seem to wrap our minds 'round."

She smiled as Charlie pulled out the chair for her and handed her a steaming cup. "So you're having a powwow about the murder?" Marian put the cup to her lips and paused, "Decaf?"

"Yep." Charlie kissed the back of her neck, causing Marian to shiver.

She closed her eyes. "Mmm, nice." Then tasted the coffee.

Luke coughed. "So, we haven't found any evidence that points to our killer. All we have is the tieback, the rosary beads, graying brown hairs, and fingerprints galore from the armoire."

"Tell me again your suspects and why. Tell me everything you know," Marian said.

Luke rattled off the names and reasons. Dylan restated his findings.

Marian twisted her mouth. "All the suspects are men? Why can't it be a jealous woman?"

The men were silent. She could see their minds working. "Ethan, the moving guy, is he married?"

"Yes, to the receptionist." Luke glanced at Charlie.

Charlie rubbed Marian's lower back. "You've got a point there, deary. Darla Jean was a tiny little thing. It wouldn't take much to strangle her and dump her in the armoire."

"Yeah, Ethan's wife could be a mover herself and she knew all about the armoire." Luke pulled on his lower lip. "And according to Scottie, he had plenty of admirers. Who knows who Darla Jean may have made jealous? And the armoire was sitting in the side entrance foyer at St. Fergus for about a week before it was picked up. Anyone entering that way would have seen it."

"What about Josephine, or the woman Thelma mentioned … Dora, yeah that's the name? Either one of them could have been jealous. You know, because Darla Jean had Scottie the Hottie wrapped around her little finger. Thelma said both were sweet on him."

The men laughed.

Marian smirked, "Hey, women can be spiteful, mean, and vicious. Believe me, you don't want to tick us off." She crossed her arms and gave them her best drop-dead look.

Dylan was leaning against the sink. He turned to rinse out his coffee mug and asked, "Was Matt seeing anyone else? And don't forget about the hairs. How many of your suspects have graying brown hair?"

Rubbing his hands across his cheeks and to the back of his neck, Charlie squeezed his shoulders and groaned. "About half of them, including Scottie's attorney."

Sean had been sitting quietly. "Guys, you keep going around in circles. And Marian made a good point." He stood and stretched. "It's getting late. I think after a good night's sleep and with a fresh mind in the morning, things will begin to gel."

"So Mr. FBI Man, who do you think did it?" Charlie slapped his older brother on the back.

He hunched up his shoulders. "Not my case. I've got too much running around in my brain to give it one thought." Sean grinned wickedly, "But give me two seconds and I'll have it solved."

"Get out of here." Charlie pushed him toward the front door.

"Oh, no, not until I say good night to Marian." He kissed her on the cheek. "She's the wisest one in the room."

"Thank you," she replied as she patted Sean's stubble-covered cheek. Marian yawned. "I'm going up." She said her goodnights and gave Charlie a quick peck on the lips.

Da followed her up the stairs. He heard his sister's snores before they reached the top. Going into the bedroom where his sister slept, Da shoved Aunt Ella. "Roll over, ol' girl. Ya keepin' our Marian awake with ya snorin'."

She rolled over without waking up. Quietness filled the room.

"Thanks, Da."

He stood with his fists on his hips and winked. "If she starts up, just give her a nudge," Da said with a pushing motion.

♣

Dylan had followed Sean out the door. Luke and Charlie sat in silence staring at the pattern in the marble-topped island.

Charlie moaned, "Augh! The answer is right there. I know it is. Why can't I see it?"

"I'm with Sean. Let's look at it in the morning. I'm beat."

"Yeah, I'm afraid we need to talk with all of the suspects again. Maybe, just maybe, Marian is right. If so, we'll have to look at everything from a new angle."

Luke yawned and stretched to his full height. "Charlie, I can't ever repay you for helping me." He clamped his brother-in-law's well-developed shoulder. "Thanks, I know you'd rather be with Marian."

He was right. Charlie wanted more than anything to be with Marian 24 hours a day. But being a copper was in his blood - something he could never deny. "Pff, you'd do the same for me. Hopefully, we'll have an answer tomorrow."

Luke rubbed his temple. A headache was threatening. He knew he would be on his knees praying beside his bed. Praying for wisdom. Praying that when this was over, he would be able to do his job without anyone's help. And he would offer a prayer of thanks for having Charlie show him the ropes. He clicked his tongue. "We can only pray. See ya in the morning."

Charlie went upstairs and paused outside of Marian's door and listened. No snoring. He smiled and trudged on to his room thinking three more days, only three more everlasting days.

Chapter 22

Officer Kitty Donovan's big brown eyes bulged as Charlie and Luke pushed through the lobby door. "Detectives O'Sullivan and McClung, you just missed Scottie. His lawyer sprung him."

"Good morning to you too, Officer Donovan," smiled McClung. "Not exactly the greeting I was looking for this morning."

The young female officer blushed. "Sorry, sir."

As he waved her away, McClung said, "Nothing to apologize about. This case has me a bit irritable. Please accept my peace offering." Charlie handed her a bag of blueberry muffins that Ma had shoved in his hand before he fled the kitchen. He remembered the ones Marian had made when they first met. Yep, Marian's were definitely tastier than Ma's. He didn't know how, but they were hands down better and he'd never tell Ma.

"Thank you, sir," Kitty grinned, feeling relieved. "Scottie left with his lawyer at eight-thirteen this morning. And here's a message for you, Detective O'Sullivan." She gave Luke a square pink note.

Luke laughed as he read it, walking toward his office. "Can you believe it? Ma reminding us to get our tuxes today, or else."

Charlie plopped down and slung his heels up on Luke's desk. "Right now, I don't know which has me more knotted up, the murder or Ma." He sighed. *Two more days. Only two more days and I'll be the happiest man in the whole universe. That is if the case is solved before*

Sunday, he thought. "Augh, you heard her giving me instructions this morning."

Luke grinned, "Yeah, I'm glad we had to leave. Ma had that look in her eyes. I love her but when she's on a mission, world beware."

Charlie dropped his feet to the floor. "You know what's funny? I think Marian is loving Ma clucking around her like a mother hen." He rubbed his earlobe. "Women! I'll never solve that mystery."

Luke rested his hand on the telephone. "Don't even go down that path. Back to the murder. I figured we'd call Matt's father and take a trip to the moving company and St. Fergus. What do you want to do about Scottie?"

"Let's go visit Thelma and Theodore to get Scottie's log book and then ..." Charlie sat in silence mulling around Marian's idea. "Then let's go talk to Dora and, after that, Ethan's wife." He stood and stretched. "We'll play it by ear after that."

♣

"You're not going to like this boys, but Scottie was nowhere near St. Fergus when Darla Jean was murdered." Theodore gave Scottie's log book to Charlie.

"Could he have forged the records?"

Thelma snaked her skinny arm around Charlie's shoulders. "I took the call myself and dispatched him to old widow Glendinning's place. She ran out of cat chow. Scottie drove Ethel to *The Quickie Mart* around midnight."

Luke slowly beat the wall with his fist. "Damn, damn, damn!"

"Are you sure about that? He really drove her there at that time?" Charlie asked.

"I called Ethel to verify it. He even paid for the cat chow. Refused to take her money and paid her fare, too, according to Ethel. She remembered the time, the witching hour she called it." Thelma squeezed Charlie's shoulders. "Sorry, I could've sworn he was the one."

He handed back the log book. "No need for this then. Thanks." Charlie puffed out his cheeks and after a slow exhale said, "Well, Luke, let's hit the pharmacy. I could use a Dr Pepper."

♣

The bell chimed as Luke and Charlie entered the pharmacy. Dora was leaning on the counter, her elbows supporting her healthy girth.

Unaware of them, her lips continued to move as she read the paperback clutched in her thick hands. A naked, well-muscled man groping a voluptuous, naked woman with her female bits covered by her long hair graced the cover of the book.

Charlie coughed. "Hello, Dora, could we get two large Dr Peppers to go?" He had to stifle a laugh when she threw the book into the air.

Dora grabbed the book as it slid across the counter and shoved it in her apron pocket. "Yeah, coming right up." She turned her back and tucked a clump of graying hair that had escaped from her long ponytail behind her ear.

Charlie and Luke sat at the counter watching Dora cram ice into the cups. "Hey, dump out about half of that ice. Thanks." Charlie shook his head.

Dora set the cups in front of them with two straws. A pale blush lingered on her cheeks. Wiping the sweat from her top lip with the back of her hand, she asked, "Can I get y'all anything else?"

Luke gave her a five. "Keep the change. Say, we need to ask you a couple of questions." He retrieved a notepad and pen.

Shoving the bill in her pocket with her spicy book, she answered, "Shoot."

Charlie began, "Did you know Darla Jean well?"

Her eyes crinkled. "Sorta, why?"

"Did you have a close relationship with Scottie?"

She backed away a few steps. "Uhh …" The blush on her cheeks grew darker. "No, I mean, he was good-lookin' and all that and uh …" she grunted, "I have to be honest … I liked his flirting. It made me feel young and attractive, but he'd never be interested in someone like me. Really? I mean look at me. Fat, old, and plain."

The bell chimed as a giggly blonde strolled in. Dora pointed toward her. "Now, Cindy there, claims to have hit a home run with him. She's the one you should be talking to."

Charlie remembered the blonde from yesterday, the one behind the counter flirting with Scottie. "Okay, but one more question. Where were you late Tuesday night between eleven-fifteen and one?

Dora scoffed, "Where I am every night at that time, in bed with my two cats and my German Shepherd at the foot of the bed. I have to get up at four in the morning to take care of them and get myself ready to open the pharmacy at six."

"What y'all doing here, again? Lookin' to pick on Scottie some more?" The blonde sneered, smacking gum like cud.

Charlie rolled his eyes and asked sarcastically, "Yeah, where is he?"

Dora slapped the blonde on her shoulder. "Cindy, show some respect. Act like you've a brain or two in that empty head."

Cindy snatched up an apron from under the counter and pouted as she tied it on. "I'm not stupid." She stuck out her tongue at Dora who walked away in frustration.

"I don't know where Scottie boy is. I ain't heard from him since y'all took him away." Cindy crossed her arms under her ample chest and scowled.

Charlie studied the defiant girl. Her dark roots needed touching up and she could go easier with the black eyeliner. "How old are you, Cindy?"

"Eighteen. I'll be nineteen next month."

Luke scribbled on the notepad and asked, "Did you know Darla Jean?"

"The dead wannabe nun? Yeah, I knew of her." Cindy chewed the gum faster.

Ah, pricked a nerve there, thought Charlie. "Seems to be a little jealousy there. Were you and Scottie going together and he began to stray?"

Cindy tossed back her head. "Hah, Scottie ain't gonna be tied down to no girl. Besides, that dead girl ain't got nuthin over me." She pushed up her crossed arms to accentuate her substantial breasts.

Charlie was tired of this game. "Fine, where were you last Tuesday night between eleven-fifteen and one?"

She grinned and winked. "I'll tell ya and ya can guess what I was doin'. Biting her lower lip, Cindy leaned over resting her forearms on the counter exposing definite cleavage. "I was in bed and I weren't alone. If ya need a name, I'll tell ya, but I don't think his wife would be too happy, causin' he was supposed to be workin' the late shift." She pushed back from the counter. "Well, ya got any more questions? I got a job to do."

Charlie wondered what kind of parents she had, or if she was just one of those kids. Maybe he was lucky he didn't have any children. "I think I've heard enough. Dora, could we get a refill?"

They walked to the car with their refills and leaned against it. Charlie looked down Main Street toward his family's antique shop and wondered what Ma had Marian doing. *No, I don't want to go there*, he thought. "I guess it's on to the moving company."

♣

"Hi! Ethan's not here. Is there something I can help you with?" the receptionist asked.

Charlie scanned her smiling perky face. She appeared to be nice and squeaky clean. "We're here to speak to you."

A puzzled looked transformed her face. "Oh, okay. Please have a seat. Do you want some coffee, anything before we get started?" She jumped up to serve them.

"Coffee would be nice, just two sugars," Luke replied.

Charlie shook his open hand. "Nothing for me, thanks."

Handing Luke a foam cup, she questioned, "Are you moving?"

Luke tasted the coffee. "Good coffee, Cheryl. No, we need to ask you a couple of questions concerning the Darla Jean Rogers murder."

"Let me get the work order. I'm sure you'll be needing that."

As Cheryl flipped through the files, Luke asked, "Did you know Darla Jean?"

Cheryl handed Luke the file. "I know her parents through the church. And we always requested a table at Darla Jean's station at *The Steakhouse*." She smiled. "Darla Jean was such a great waitress. Best customer service ever. Ethan always left her a big tip." With a sigh, Cheryl added, "She'll definitely be missed."

Luke passed the file to Charlie.

"So the only interaction you had with Darla Jean was at *The Steakhouse*?" Charlie asked. He noticed on the paperwork that Josephine had ordered the pickup of the armoire. "Josephine Mendel, Father Eli's sister, made all the arrangements for the armoire?"

"Yes to both of your questions."

"What was your husband's relationship with Darla Jean?" Luke asked.

Cheryl frowned, "There was no relationship other than customer and waitress. What are you insinuating, Luke? Ethan is a decent man. An honest man. You should know better than to ask me a question like that. Really?"

Charlie answered for his embarrassed brother-in-law. "Please take no offense at Officer O'Sullivan's question. It's a standard question in a murder investigation, like the question I'm about to ask. Where were you and your husband late Tuesday night between eleven-fifteen and one?"

She swallowed hard. "I'm sorry if I overreacted. It's just my husband is a friendly man. I know how rumors can get started in a small town, especially for newcomers like us. But to answer your question, we were in bed asleep. Ethan had a full schedule on Wednesday and we wanted to get an early start, so we were in bed by ten."

"Thank you, you've been very helpful. I believe those are all the questions we have for now." Charlie held the folder. "Would you mind making copies of the paperwork for us?"

Cheryl grinned. "You're the detective the whole town's been buzzing about for the past three months, aren't you? You're getting married Sunday."

Nodding he answered, "Yep, I'm the one. You're invited to the wedding. I think Ma expects the whole town to attend. You know Ma, right?"

"Oh, yes, she's delightful! Ma made us feel right at home when we moved here a little over a year ago."

Luke took the copies from Cheryl. "I didn't mean to upset you. I hope you know that."

She waved away his apology. "I've already forgotten about it."

Stepping outside, Charlie's stomach rumbled. "What do you say about lunch?"

"Let's do the tux thing first, we'll be killed if we forget."

Charlie tapped his temple. "You're a wise man. Tux, lunch, and then Matt."

♣

Fitted and fed, Charlie and Luke entered a small house at the end of Main Street that served as the law office of David Hoffsteader. They were welcomed by a stern secretary. Her tightly-woven French twist seemed to pull her eyes back into slits as she peered at them over her reading glasses.

She stood as she greeted them. "Gentlemen, you must be the two detectives Mr. Hoffsteader is expecting. Will you please follow me to the conference room?"

They followed her short, quick steps down the hallway. The secretary pointed to a sideboard with freshly brewed coffee and iced lemonade. "Please make yourselves comfortable. Mr. Hoffsteader should be with you shortly. Do you require anything before I leave?"

They both shook their heads and answered "no."

"Very well." She shut the door behind her.

Charlie poured a glass of lemonade while Luke had another cup of coffee. "David must be doing well." Charlie looked around at the room's teak wood furniture, the rich Persian rug, and original artwork. He ran a moist finger around the edge of the delicate glass. It began to sing, proving it was crystal."

Luke looked at the bottom of his dainty cup. "Yep, I'd say so. Royal Copenhagen."

The door opened. David was followed by Matt. "Gentlemen, please be seated. I hope we can make this brief."

"This will be so brief there'll be no need to sit down," confirmed Charlie and addressed his questions to David Hoffsteader. "First, was Matthew dating any other girls? If so, did they know about his relationship with Darla Jean?"

Matthew sat down and his father stood behind him. "Matthew was not seeing anyone else in town. Anyone he may have seen at college knew nothing about Darla Jean and had never visited Mercy City. Next question."

"Where were you and your wife late Tuesday night between eleven-fifteen and one?"

David stared at Charlie. "Why are you asking me that question? Surely you don't think I, or my wife, have anything to do with this."

Charlie shrugged. "You said you didn't see your son come home. Was that because you weren't at home?" He placed the delicate crystal on the fine teak sideboard then stood within arm's length of David. "I thought maybe you didn't like the idea of Darla Jean carrying your son's bastard child. Maybe she was blackmailing you?"

"What? Why would she blackmail me? If she had approached me, I would have sued her for sole custody of my grandchild. I would have dragged her through the mud to get my grandchild. Damn her good girl reputation!"

That response squashed one of his theories unless David was an exceptional actor. But on the other hand, Matthew looked as if all of the blood had been drained from his face. Charlie could almost hear the wheels churning in the boy's brain as sweat beaded on his forehead from the effort.

"She was screwing around with everybody and anybody. How would I know if that baby was mine? Hell, it could be that damn taxi driver's for all I know. Or Father Eli's." Matt's eyes bulged. "Oh, yeah, she had the hots for him real bad."

David Hoffsteader inhaled deeply, assuming his "cool as a cucumber" defense attorney facade. "I take it the paternity test verified that Matthew is the father of the child?"

Charlie and Luke nodded.

Matt rested his head on the oval conference table and uttered no sound.

Charlie wondered if Matt's reaction was a sign of defeat. "Was she blackmailing you, Matt? Is that why you killed Darla Jean?"

Silence.

"Son, answer the question honestly. I will get you out of this. Trust me."

Charlie snorted softly. *How in the world did David think he could get his son out of a murder rap?*

"Nooo, I didn't kill her." Matt sat up suddenly and hit the table with his fist. "Why don't you believe me? I didn't kill her." All the blood had returned to his beet-red face. Slamming his fist on the table one more time, Matthew groaned, "I didn't."

"Did she want money from you?" asked Luke.

Matthew nodded.

"How much and when did she want it?" Charlie asked. "Did she want you to marry her? What were her plans for the baby and herself?"

Matt ran his hand around his mouth. Pushing his chair back, he went to the sideboard for lemonade. "She was going to have the baby. The nuns knew about it and were going to help her adopt it out. Darla wanted money to help with expenses until the baby was adopted. She wanted the money yesterday, one hundred thousand dollars."

Charlie tugged his earlobe. "So let me get this right. She was going to join the convent, have the baby, and give it up for adoption. Darla Jean had no interest in marrying you or keeping the baby. All she wanted from you was money."

Pouring a glass of lemonade, Matt nodded. "Yep, she said she had no interest in me whatsoever. All she needed from me was cash."

"Son, why didn't you come to me for help?" David sat down and looked as if sadness had swallowed him.

"She didn't want anyone to know. She wanted everyone to think she was a good girl. She said it would kill her parents to know she was less than a saint." Matt grunted, "Darla Jean was far from that. I mean come on. A pregnant nun?" He looked at his father, "I was going to ask you for the money, but she was killed before I could."

Charlie paced around the table. "Why did you go back to her house? Why follow her to the church?"

"The thing is, as I was driving away I knew I couldn't come up with that kind of money. I would have to ask Dad for it. I had to explain that to her. When I met up with her at the church and told her I had to tell my father, she flew into a rage. She didn't want her reputation tainted. I left, hoping by the morning she'd come to her senses. That we could work out something. But we didn't get the chance."

Chapter 23

Today is her funeral. Such a shame she had to die. But what other choice did I have? Darla Jean always wanted more. She had to have it all. Didn't she know that's impossible? I guess you can say she died trying. That phrase amuses me now. But I shouldn't laugh. Not in God's house, but then again, He does have a sense of humor. I mean look at the platypus. Now that's funny.

I love becoming one with the shadows in the church. It's like I'm an actual part of its soul. Hidden in the darkness, I can see what God sees. The sinners coming and going from His house. I hear their breathing and feel their pain as they weep. And at times, I can sense their joy. But I know their joy won't last. It never does. Something or someone will make it bitter and it will wither away like rotten fruit.

No! I don't want these feelings of anger, of loss, and of envy to consume my peace of being one with God. I need to pray. I need to seek forgiveness for what I've done. It was wrong. I know it was wrong. But … it felt so right at the time.

I'm so tired of running away from myself. Tired of people telling me what to do and when to do it. And who I should love and not love. Why can't they just all leave me alone? All I want is to be one with God. He makes me feel … wanted. Yeah, wanted. He doesn't need me. What would He need me to do for Him? He can do anything. He doesn't use me like everyone else does. They say, 'I wouldn't know what I'd do without you'. Yeah, right! They would find someone else to take my place. I'm nothing more to them than a tool. But God wants me. All He wants is to love me and for me to love Him back.

Love. I should be happy with His love. His love should be the only love I need. The only love I should want. I'm ashamed to confess that I long for the warmth of arms wrapped around me. Someone's breath upon my neck as they tell me they love me. But I can't! I can't love the way I want to love. God, please take away this hunger, this craving, this need. Take away this void, this unending ache.

Her parents are walking down the center aisle. I do feel pity for them. They thought she was a good girl. She used to be a good girl, but something happened when she went to college. Still the same girl, but her thinking detoured, her definition of morality went awry. Oh, the sorrow and shame she would have plagued them with if she had lived. I did them a favor. Saved them from discovering her true nature. I did this whole town a service by ridding them of her sinful ways.

She was nothing but a user, a taker, a fraud. It just dawned on me. I did her a favor, as well. She wanted to be a good girl. She didn't want her reputation tarnished. So in essence, I saved her. The whole town still thinks of her as a good girl.

I look at Jesus hanging on the cross above the altar. My Savior. He has forgiven me. I can feel it, the peace and serenity of absolution of my terrible deed. He has shown me that I was her savior.

But it will have to be my secret. The police can't comprehend there being more than one savior. They don't have a clue. They thought they had it solved. Pff! I have them fooled. They don't understand that God works in mysterious ways. But I do. I'm God's little helper.

Chapter 24

Marian entered the church with the McClung family. She didn't know Darla Jean, but her new family was close to her parents. The last funeral she attended was Lee's, her husband. His parents sat beside her but did little to console her. It was as if they were the only ones who had suffered and she was merely someone who lived with their son, a roommate. Her brother and sister-in-law tried their best to comfort her, but she was beyond reach.

When all was said and done, she was alone. There was nothing anyone could say or do to ease the pain of death of her beloved husband. It had been just the two of them for 19 years. Then in the blink of an eye, half of her world had been cruelly ripped away leaving a gaping wound, raw and jagged. Just when she thought the scab was complete, a memory would creep in and peel it away.

Marian felt a haunting ache for her losses, first her special friend Marcia in high school, then both of her parents, then Lee, and lastly, Dianne. With the last death, she met Charlie. She smiled as she remembered how she thought he was rude when she first laid eyes on him. And now she thought he was the most practically perfect man alive. *God works in strange ways,* she thought, and said a silent prayer.

Not wanting to dwell on the past or the present, she let her mind wander around St. Fergus. This was the first time she'd really had a chance to discover the beauty of the cathedral. The stained glass murals were glorious. She turned to look at the back. The sanctuary was filling up. Charlie and Luke sat in the very last pew, watching everyone who entered. The far back corners were dark and hidden by the massive arched columns supporting the roof.

Somber organ music filled the church, bringing her back to the present. Marian imagined what Darla Jean's mother would be thinking. Was she remembering the happy times she had with her daughter when they attended mass together as a family? Or maybe it was the day Darla Jean was baptized, or had her first communion, or the day she was confirmed. Marian heard Darla Jean's mother's gut-wrenching sobs. Happy memories couldn't take away the fact that her baby girl was dead.

Marian felt guilty that in two days this same sanctuary would be a place of joy and celebration. She could feel the tears building as she remembered the pain and anger she had felt with each death she had endured. No! This was not her loss. She had had enough of death, enough of loneliness and heartache. All she wanted now was a life full of hope, love, and togetherness. No matter how insensitive it was, Marian refused to let the sadness take away her peace and happiness. She concentrated on the funeral mass and when the sadness tried to break in, she would make a mental list of things to do for the wedding.

After the funeral, family and friends gathered on the front steps of St. Fergus. Charlie slid his arm around Marian's narrow waist and kissed her temple. "Are you okay?"

She nodded with a weak smile, "Yeah, I'm fine."

He kissed her temple again. "Luke and I are going to the cemetery." Charlie looked at his parents. "And you?"

Ma blotted the corners of her eyes. "No, son, we're going home. Still got things to do for the weddin'." She blew her nose. "Now, don't ya be staying out late and neglecting ya Marian. I expect the both of you to be home for supper by six." Ma pointed to Charlie and Luke. "Don't ya be disappointing ya Ma."

Ma entwined her arm with Marian's. "Come now, my pet, I promised ya Aunt Ella we'd stop by with a bite of lunch."

Marian squeezed Charlie's hand before Ma pulled them apart. She looked over her shoulder and blew him a kiss. He caught it, touched it to his lips and then tucked it into his breast pocket over his heart.

♣

Charlie had relinquished Marian to Ma and watched her disappear around the corner with his family. *Man, I want to be with her. This case must end now.* Sighing heavily, he looked at Luke, "Let's go do some surveillance at the cemetery."

"Do you really think it'll give us any more clues?"

Charlie shook his head. "Probably not, but we've got to do it just in case."

There weren't many cars lined up to follow the hearse to the graveside. Charlie was grateful. Fingers crossed, maybe he'd be home early. And just as he predicted, the cemetery provided nothing but sore feet from standing so long on the hard ground.

On the drive home, Luke and Charlie went over the suspect list. The original list consisted of three: Matthew Hoffsteader, Scottie the Hottie, and Father Eli. Then they added Ethan and his wife to the list, as well as Dora. But now Matthew, Scottie, Dora, Ethan and his wife had been crossed off. Which left only Father Eli.

Luke shook his head. "No, I just can't believe Father Eli had anything to do with Darla Jean's murder."

"You can't rule out him," Charlie insisted. "If Darla Jean was blackmailing Father Eli, you don't know what he would do to protect his reputation. She wanted a hundred thousand dollars from Matt. Maybe the money from the sale of the armoire wasn't enough for her."

Luke grunted. "I know you're right. He had the opportunity and maybe a motive."

"I don't want to discuss this anymore. We have tomorrow to worry about it. Let's talk about anything besides that," muttered Charlie.

"All right, Scarlett, tomorrow is another day," Luke chuckled. "I know what'll put a smile on your face … the honeymoon."

A huge grin split Charlie's sour face. "Ya damn straight about that!"

♣

The aroma of fried chicken made Charlie's stomach grumble as he walked in the front door of his parents' home. He hurried into the kitchen. Ma and Marian were standing at the cooktop. Each manned a cast iron skillet turning pieces of chicken as the grease sizzled and popped. Charlie stood watching them sway as they cooked and sang the Irish ditty, *Side by Side*.

Charlie applauded when they finished, bellowing with laughter. "You sound like angels."

Marian turned. The flour that was smeared on her face seemed to enhance her lovely smile. "Oh, Charlie, you're home early." She ran into his arms, giving him a generous kiss. "Is it over?" she asked anxiously.

He wiped the flour from her cheeks, "No, but we're closing in. No talk about that tonight. I want to hear all about the wedding plans."

Ma answered, "Ya both sit down. Supper will be in a bit. I'll get ya tea and scones."

"Ma, you sit. You've been on your feet all day." Marian led her to sit next to Charlie at the big kitchen island. "I can get the tea and scones."

Charlie hugged Ma. "She's a keeper. What do you think?"

Ma was in awe of how perfect a woman Marian was for her son. He had gone through some doozies, but he listened to his granny's advice. The boy is patient, she thought. "Great things come to those who wait, son." She patted his cheek. "Aye, she's a keeper, that she is indeed."

Luke inhaled deeply as he entered. "I love me some fried chicken." He plopped next to Ma. Watching Marian fuss around the kitchen, he snorted, "I see you've trained her well."

Ma didn't retort to his comment but gave Luke a playful poke with her elbow.

Marian set a cup of tea in front of Luke. She stared into his eyes. "Ah, yes, she also taught me how not to take any guff from you men." She grinned, "I'd be careful drinking that tea."

Luke pushed away the cup.

"Son, she just meant it's hot." Ma winked at Marian. "But I'd watch ya back. She's a feisty one."

Chapter 25

The McClung Clan sat around the table discussing the wedding plans. The kids were clearing the dishes. The mischievous sounds of joking and threats of being popped with a dish towel could be heard from the kitchen.

Luke whispered in Rachel's ear, "You may want to have a backup plan for Father Eli."

Her head whipped around. Rachel studied her husband's face looking for a twinkle of a tease. There was none. He was serious. "You mean …?" Her fingertips pressed her lips as she swallowed hard. *Not Father Eli*, she willed, *not Father Eli*.

Rachel looked around the table. Everyone was engrossed in the wedding plans. She left without being noticed. Luke followed her out to the front porch.

"Oh, Luke, if you're right, this will ruin everything. Can you wait until after the wedding?"

Luke leaned against the railing. "Charlie wants this solved before the wedding. Doesn't want it hanging around in his mind during the honeymoon, if you know what I mean?"

Her shoulders fell with a big sigh. Rachel knew exactly what he meant. Nothing happening in the bedroom. "Are you sure it's Father Eli? I mean really sure? I thought Scottie was the one."

He sat on the porch steps. "No, we're not sure. But the suspect list is whittling down to him."

She joined him and gripped his knee. "What's your gut telling you?"

"Father Eli's not the one."

The screen door groaned as the family said their goodnights and left. Ma and Da stood at the door. "Don't ya boys be up all night. Tomorrow's goin' to be a busy day. Lots to do before the big day and ya gotta be gettin' up before the sun."

Rachel and Luke stood, giving them a kiss. "Yes, Ma, Rach and I'll be leaving soon. Goodnight."

Charlie and Marian sat on the steps as Rachel and Luke joined them.

"I think you're right, Luke. I don't think Father Eli did it either," Charlie confirmed. "There's something nagging in the back of my mind." He grasped the air. "But I just can't ..." Charlie moaned and ran his hands over his head.

"What about her mother?" Marian asked. "Or the boy's mother."

They all looked at her as if she had snakes for hair.

"Ah, come on. It's possible." She shifted to face them all. "What I mean is ... well, I keep hearing what a good girl Darla Jean was. But she wasn't, right?"

"Yeah, so?" Charlie answered curiously. He wanted to see where her slippery trail was leading.

"Only a handful of people know her true nature. What if Darla Jean confessed to her mother? And she was so mortified to learn that her precious, adorable, saint of a daughter was nothing but a conniving, excuse my crude term, tramp, who used everyone, that her mother wanted to ..." Marian put her hands into the air as if she was squeezing something. "Choke her. So no one would ever find out. Heck, even her dad could've done it for the same reasons."

Charlie bobbed his head in agreement. "Mmm, possible, just possible. What's your theory on Matt's mom?"

"Well, sort of the same thing except she didn't want her son forced into marrying Darla Jean. You said he didn't love her." Marian snapped her fingers. "Or maybe she was afraid Darla Jean would dump the baby on them and she didn't want to raise a bastard grandchild." She slumped back with a grin, satisfied with her hypotheses.

Luke shook his head. "No, Matt's dad said they would have raised the baby."

Marian sat up quickly. "That's what he said, but what if mom was looking forward to an empty nest or was ready to make her own life without anybody in it? You know, skip town. And you could say the same thing for Darla Jean's mother."

"You've got some devious thoughts in there." Charlie ruffled her hair.

Rachel smirked. "I don't know about that. I could never do a thing like that to one of my kids. Besides, her parents are pretty torn up."

Luke nodded in agreement.

"Here goes my warped mind again." Marian stood and paced on the ground while she formed another theory. "We never really know people, or how their minds work. All we see is the person they present to us." She pointed to Rachel. "You know how you would react, but not everyone will react the same as you, right?"

"Okay, yes."

Marian continued. "So maybe they were so torn up, not only because Darla Jean is dead, but because they killed her and they are afraid they will be caught. Or maybe they are horrified by the knowledge that they are capable of killing their own child."

She stopped pacing and sat next to Charlie and mumbled, "I read too many murder novels, don't I?"

He pulled her close and felt her shivering. "Are you cold?"

Marian shook her head. "Nerves, I think."

Charlie rubbed the goosebumps on her arm. "You bring a fresh perspective to the table. Keep reading your books. Maybe one day you'll make me into a fine detective."

"I don't think I would have ever looked at it that way but you know, she makes a good argument," Luke pointed out.

Charlie rested his chin on top of Marian's head. "Yeah. I guess we need to revisit the parents after we speak with Father Eli." He wondered if that was the thing that had been eluding him. Frowning, it still didn't feel right. Maybe he was too tired to think about it. Maybe in the morning, he would see things more clearly.

He stood, pulling Marian up with him. "No more murderous thoughts. Time to go to bed. Remember tomorrow is going to be non-stop."

Marian's knee popped as she stood. "Yeah, I can already feel it in my old bones."

Laughing, Rachel hugged her soon to be sister-in-law. "I should have warned you about Ma. She doesn't do anything halfway. No sir, it's to the max."

"I wouldn't have it any other way," sighed Marian.

♣

Marian lay in the twin bed, awakened by Aunt Ella's constant soft snoring. When she first entered the bedroom, Marian had accidently, on purpose, bumped the vanity chair. Its bang had stopped the snoring for a little while. Just long enough to allow Marian to fall asleep.

She wondered if Charlie snored. The thought made her nervous. A man in her bed after 11 years of sleeping alone. It hadn't taken her long to get used to sleeping alone after Lee died. Being a long-haul pilot, he would be gone for days at a time, sometimes weeks. Charlie would be with her every night.

Every night. Marian mulled it around. Since she and Charlie met three months ago, they had seen each other almost every day either at lunch or dinner, depending on their schedules, so it wouldn't be a hard adjustment to make.

After Chief Perry Miller was arrested, Charlie had been asked to fill in. He thought he might be asked to take the job permanently. No one else at the station expressed any interest in assuming the responsibilities as chief. Marian wanted him to take the job in hopes of keeping him safer. And it would almost be dependable office hours.

So much had changed in those three months. She was a grieving widow and now a blushing bride-to-be. Her mind began to spin.

Where were they going to live? Charlie lived in a two-bedroom condo. No, she couldn't live there. She needed more space.

Marian laughed softly. Her house, situated on half an acre of land, was almost 4,000 square feet, including the patio and screened porch. Why did she, living all alone, need that much? Then she remembered that the zoning restrictions on her neighborhood required all homes be a minimum of 3,500 square feet. And it was the change she needed after Lee died. Something totally opposite of her life with him. Although it was a wonderful life, her life without Lee would never be the same no matter how hard she tried.

Since the night she was almost killed in her very own house, she had been living with Joan. The house was being remodeled after the extensive damage that was done in the master bedroom and bath. But she was having the whole house redone, not wanting any reminders of that night. The house would be finished by the time they returned home.

Well, it's like our house. Charlie has been consulted on every decision I've made with the remodel. Yes, we'll live there since it's a totally new house inside, she decided. Then she worried if Charlie would think she was being overbearing by telling him where he would live. She decided they could talk about it while on their honeymoon.

Oh, the honeymoon. She panicked. It will be like the first time all over again, but worse. It wouldn't be the first time for either of them. She wondered what he expected. *Stop it*! Marian screamed silently to herself. Taking deep breaths, she began to calm down telling herself when the time comes to just go with the flow. Follow his lead.

Another one of her mother's favorite sayings came to mind. No need to worry. It's like a rocking chair, keeps you occupied, but doesn't get you anywhere. Right. She would tackle each decision when needed. And the honeymoon was two nights' away. The decision she needed to make tomorrow was where to shop for the proper honeymoon lingerie. Marian decided to ask Sarah about that.

Tomorrow was definitely going to be a busy day with so many things to accomplish. She needed to sleep—sleep she wouldn't have as long as Aunt Ella continued to snore. Tip-toeing close to Aunt Ella, she reached for her shoulder and gently rolled her onto her side. Silence. Sweet, sweet silence. Marian returned to bed and prayed for restful slumber.

Chapter 26

Charlie woke with a start. Looking around the room, he remembered he was in his old room in his parents' home. The dream disturbed his sleep. He could see the killer hiding in shadows. Stepping into the darkness, Charlie heard the killer's breathing. He looked around but could see nothing in the blackness. Reaching out, he grabbed in the direction of the sound only to find nothing, just taunting laughter as the killer evaded capture.

The shadows were cold and oppressive. He wanted to escape. No matter which direction, or how far he ventured, there was no way out. Sweat ran down his temples and down his neck. The laughter was moving away so he followed it. The blackness turned to gray. He continued toward the mocking laughter. A tiny round speck of light pierced the shadows dancing away from him. Charlie could see freedom just ahead of the speck of light.

He stepped into the bright sunlight. Its rays warmed his skin. He was free, but not from the laughter. It bounced around from all sides. Cold sweat drowned him as he saw Marian walking toward the shadows. He called her name as she reached into the shadows. She turned and smiled at him. The sunlight glinted off a small golden loop in her left earlobe. A skeletal hand slithered from the darkness. Marian didn't see it. Her eyes were fixed on him. With one swift tug, she disappeared into the shadows. NOOOOO!

Charlie jumped from the bed and hurried to her bedroom. Opening the door, he saw Marian safe in bed asleep. "Thank you, God." He murmured as he shut the door. His fear was like that night. The night he thought Diane's murderer had killed Marian. His heart still pounding from the dream, he went to the kitchen for water.

He held the glass filled with ice water to his forehead. The dream. Was it just a nightmare or was it trying to tell him something? The water soothed his throat, dry from the heavy panting caused by the skeletal hand. Charlie watched the sweat droplets trickle down the clear glass. Their paths were random, crisscrossing until they pooled onto the marble countertop.

"Where are all the clues leading me?" he asked himself as he refilled the glass. Charlie stood staring at the still twinkling stars through the kitchen windows and wondered if he would be able to put an end to this case. Sighing, he dropped his head and prayed for the answer today. The only thing he wanted occupying his mind tomorrow was Marian, only Marian. He grinned, "Yep, tomorrow."

"Who ya talkin' to son?"

Charlie's hand jerked at the sudden sound of Ma's voice. Water splashed on his face and bare chest. "Ma, you scared the—."

Ma had a towel in her hand to dry her son but instead, she covered his mouth. "Now, watcha language. You made enough noise to be wakin' the dead. What's botherin' ya, son?"

He shook his head and kissed Ma's cheek. "Nothing to be worrying your pretty little head about. I know you don't like copper talk first thing in the morning." Charlie looked at the clock, almost 4:30. "You're up earlier than usual."

"Tah, too much preying on my mind. Let me fix us up somethin' to eat. What'd ya say, just the two of us?"

He loved Ma and would do most anything to make her happy. Charlie knew Ma expressed her love through food. Luckily, she was a magnificent cook. Marian and Joan were just a frog's hair away from her. "Sure, Ma, but don't go crazy. I can't eat a proper fry-up this early."

She rolled her eyes. "When do I ever go crazy?"

Charlie started the coffee. "Tah, ya don't be wantin' me to be answerin' that now, do ya?" He said in an Irish brogue.

Ma waved him away. "Don't ya be teasin' to ya poor ol' ma." She opened cupboards, pulled out pans, and gathered the food to begin her magic.

♣

The smell of coffee and bacon teased Marian awake. It was dark outside. She looked at her watch laying on the nightstand. *5 o'clock! Who's up cooking at this hour?* Aunt Ella was on her back snoring. Quietly, she put on her robe and slippers.

Marian leaned against the kitchen archway. Charlie and Ma chattered while they stirred pots and flipped eggs and bacon. A box of strawberries on the island waited to be washed and sliced. A sense of regret eased into her thoughts. All these years, she had been missing this. Her life before now seemed hollow. She assumed she had been happy until this. Now she knew the true meaning of the words: family, love, and togetherness. *My life was good but not whole. And now? Now it is complete,* she decided.

Charlie and Ma were in a world of their own, unaware of her presence. She watched as they worked as a team preparing breakfast. Her heart swelled with joy as she witnessed the love between mother and son. Marian recalled her mother's advice. The way a man treats his mother is the way he will treat his wife. At this moment, she felt like the most blessed woman alive.

"Marian! How long have you been standing there?" Charlie laid a big spoon on a saucer. He wrapped his arms around her. "Are you all right? You look like you're in a trance."

She squeezed him. "I'm more than all right." Kissing his unshaven cheek, she asked, "Did you cook enough for me?"

"Sit, my pet. We've enough to feed the whole clan," replied Ma. "You'll be needin' ya strength to get through this day. We've loads of things to accomplish before the big day."

Charlie stood at the sink, washing and slicing the strawberries. He dropped a few on the steaming oatmeal Ma had placed in front of her. Handing Marian a honey jar, he instructed her to drizzle some on the oatmeal. Then he poured cream into it.

"Now stir all together and take a bite." He watched her mix the concoction and sample it. "How is it? More cream or honey?"

She shook her head. "This is good. It tastes a little different. What did you put in it?"

Charlie and Ma exchanged a sly grin.

Ma placed on the island a platter of bacon, eggs, and hash browns along with a basket of homemade biscuits, just out of the oven, then she answered, "Whiskey."

"What? Whiskey in oatmeal? For breakfast?" Marian laughed.

Charlie smiled. "But you like it don't you?"

"Yep." Marian spooned more into her mouth.

Ma winked and rubbed Charlie's back. "Aye, son. Ya got a keeper there."

Within a few minutes, Da joined them, followed closely by Aunt Ella.

"When's the rest of the family arriving?" asked Da as he slid bacon and eggs onto his plate.

Ma squinted and tilted her head. "The girls should be here soon and the boys won't be around 'til suppertime. They've a sports thing or something."

As if on cue, Sarah, Emma, and Rachel entered with their girls.

"Well, speak of the devil," Da greeted them. "Where's ya lazy husbands, now?"

Sarah kissed Ma. "Sean and Luke are right behind. Dylan's making rounds at the hospital."

The kitchen buzzed with activity. Charlie pulled Marian aside. "Here," he gave her a mug of coffee. "Let's sit on the porch swing while they finish with breakfast."

Marian nestled against Charlie's side. "This is nice. But tomorrow will be nicer."

"Mmm. If we can get through this day without Ma working us to death."

They sat in silence listening to the sounds around them. The birds singing, the swing creaking, and the ruckus from inside the house.

Charlie took Marian's empty mug and set it next to his on the porch rail. "Had a bad dream last night involving you. Promise me you will stay out of trouble."

She started to laugh, but she saw the seriousness of the request in his eyes. "I promise, but I don't see how I could get into trouble with Ma glued to my hip."

Pulling Marian to his chest, he gently held her and kissed the top of her head. "Just keep your eyes open. I've waited too long for you to lose you now." He bent his head and kissed her like it would be the last time. "I love you, Marian Frances soon-to-be McClung, with all of the life within me."

She felt his heart thumping against her breast. Tears threatened. Never would she doubt the love that Charlie had for her. This man that held her was more than she deserved. All she wanted was to make him happy.

Suddenly, Charlie held her out from him and brushed Marian's hair away from her ears. A sigh of relief passed from his lips when he saw nothing in her earlobes. "Oh, good, no gold loops." He tapped his finger against her lips. "And don't wear any. Promise me."

Marian's brows furrowed. "What did you dream last night?"

"Just promise me to be aware of your surroundings, okay?"

She kissed the tip of his finger, then crossed her heart with it. "Promise."

"Ma said to get your behinds in the house. There's work to be done," yelled Emma.

Charlie yelled back, "Be there in a minute." He heard Emma stomping away. He kissed Marian passionately. "There, that should hold you until tonight."

Marian caught her breath. "Wow! I should say so. I felt that down to my toes."

Chapter 27

Charlie yawned. "Sorry, I had a rough night. Bad dreams. This murder's got me … I don't know." He stared out the windshield as Luke drove to the Rogers' house.

"Sounds like a stop at the pharmacy for coffee. It's still kinda early to be banging on their door anyway."

"No argument from me." Charlie dreaded questioning Becky Rogers about her relationship with Darla Jean. The longer they could delay it the better. But it had to be done today. Why couldn't it have been Scottie?

He trailed behind Luke as they entered the pharmacy. Dora greeted them with a smile. Cindy sneered and informed Dora that she was taking a break. She disappeared out the side door.

"What's happened to your brother-in-law, Luke?" Dora watched Charlie heave up on the counter stool with a tired groan and cradled his head in his hands.

"Work," replied Luke.

Dora shoved a cup of coffee underneath Charlie's face. "This should help. Cindy still doesn't have the hang of makin' coffee. It'll put more hair on your chest."

He stared at the blackness of the coffee in the stark white mug. It reminded him of the shadow in his nightmare. Charlie usually took his coffee *straight* as Marian called it but he didn't like the weird thought of drinking the shadow and asked for creamer. Charlie watched the coffee turn the color of caramel. Sipping it, he decided maybe Marian was right about half-n-half.

"Well, Miss Dora, got any rumors that may interest us?" Luke asked.

Dora wiped the spotless Formica countertop. "Mmm, I hear tell Matthew Hoffsteader is gettin' ready to head back to college. Gonna live in a dorm off campus. And his mother is going to some spa retreat in Arizona when he leaves."

Charlie perked up. "Really, for how long?"

Dora leaned sideways against the counter. "The rumor is until she feels like comin' back."

Charlie and Luke shared the same thought. *Maybe Marian was right.*

"But that ain't all I hear." Dora looked around for anyone who may be within earshot. Lowering her voice, she added, "And the Rogers may be puttin' their house up for sale."

Charlie grunted, "Is that right? Anything else of interest?"

Dora refilled their cups. "Nothing as interestin' as that. Seems like Father Eli and Josephine had a big spat this mornin' after mass. But that's not really news. Josephine always seems to have a bee in her bonnet."

Cindy strolled up and smirked. "The woman needs to get laid. Then she wouldn't be all sour-faced all the time." She nodded slowly with a wicked grin. "Puts a smile on my face every time."

"Shut your filthy mouth." Dora hit her with a damp dishtowel. "Go slice that chocolate cake and get ready for the old timers comin' in for the early lunch special."

Cindy shrugged and rolled her tongue around the inside of her mouth. "Ain't the truth nasty sometimes?" She ambled toward the cake to be sliced.

"Humph, the girl's low-class," Dora said in disgust.

Charlie drained the mug and put his hand over the top when Dora tried to refill it. "I'd rather have a Dr Pepper with light ice. And make it a large one, the biggest cup you have."

As Dora filled a cup with soda, she spoke over her shoulder to them. "Haven't seen Scottie since y'all stopped by the last time. But he's still around. I hear he's notched down his libido to simmer."

She set down the giant foam cup in front of Charlie, then put a lid on it and handed him a straw. "Y'all must've put the fear of God into him," Dora laughed. "Gotta tell ya, I miss his flirtin'."

"That ain't what I miss," scoffed Cindy as she licked chocolate frosting from her fingertips.

Dora rolled her eyes.

Charlie made a mental note to ask who cut the pies and cakes before he ordered a piece. "Got anything else of interest?" He shook the cup. It was already half empty.

"Nah," Dora answered as she refilled Charlie's cup. "Nothing that would pertain to Darla Jean, that is."

Luke stood. "Well, Charlie, are you energized and ready to face the world?"

"Ready as I'm going to be."

Charlie handed Dora a twenty. "Mighty fine customer service. Keep the change, Dora, you've earned it."

She grinned. "My pleasure. Stop by anytime."

♣

Luke parked in the Rogers' driveway. Jason was sitting on the front porch with a glass of what looked like iced tea.

"Good morning, Jason. Mind if we sit with you for a bit?" Charlie asked.

Jason shook his head.

Luke sat in one of the chairs beside him, while Charlie pulled one in front of Jason. Charlie took the glass from Jason's hand and smelled it. It wasn't iced tea. Charlie gave the tall whiskey on the rocks to Luke.

"Listen to me, Jason." Charlie snapped his fingers. "Jason, you can't be drinking this early in the day. Where's Becky?"

Jason's eyes slowly moved from his empty hand to Charlie. Tears spilled down his unshaven face. He stared, unable to comprehend the words.

"Becky! Jason where is Becky?" Charlie sensed something wasn't right. "Luke stay here with him. I'm going in to look for Becky."

The house was like a tomb. His footsteps echoed on the bare hardwood floors. The living room was empty and the kitchen sink was full of dirty dishes. Charlie was confused. Why hadn't Josephine or somebody stopped by to check on them?

He knocked on the closed bedroom door. "Becky? Becky, are you in there? Are you okay?" Charlie put his ear to the door. Nothing. He tested the doorknob. It turned and he pushed open the door.

A disheveled Becky lay on her back on the far side of the bed. Her eyes were closed and her mouth was open. Charlie couldn't see a rise in her chest. Panic smacked him full force.

He ran to her. "BECKY!" An empty prescription bottle lay on the nightstand. Charlie put an open palm in front of her mouth and two fingers on her neck. She was still alive, but just barely.

"LUKE! GET IN HERE, NOW!" Charlie heard the screen door bang against the house and slam shut as Luke ran inside. Charlie dialed 9-1-1.

"Is she alive?" Luke asked as he checked for her pulse.

"Yeah." Charlie spied a vase full of water with dead flowers beside it. "Throw that water on her. It might help her come around."

Luke and Charlie did everything they could think of to bring Becky out of her stupor. Patting her cheeks, rubbing her wrists, and shaking her shoulders. They heard a few soft moans, then nothing.

"Is she dead yet?" Jason supported his weight against the doorframe. He was drinking the whiskey.

Charlie glared at him. "You knew she did this." He took four long strides and grabbed Jason by his shoulders. "Didn't you?"

Jason nodded as he put the glass to his lips. His trembling hands splashed whiskey down his chin.

Charlie took the glass from Jason's hand. His emotions were conflicting: anger, disbelief, and sympathy. He wanted to smash the glass on Jason's head, but at the same time he could feel the man's pain and wanted to console him.

Jason collapsed to the floor, weeping. He pulled his knees to his chest. Wrapping his arms around them, he rocked himself and moaned continually, "Nooo, nooo."

The distant sirens became louder. Charlie could hear men shouting, equipment banging, and feet running into the house. "Back here," Charlie yelled as he pulled Jason to his feet and out of the way. Leaving Luke to answer the EMT's questions, he dragged Jason to the kitchen and began to make coffee.

Sergeant Mike Purvis entered the kitchen. Jason's upper body was sprawled on the dinette table. "What's wrong with him?" He put his hand on Jason's back. Leaning down, he whispered in his ear, "Come on buddy. Talk to me. Everything's gonna be all right."

Jason's head wobbled from side to side. Drool pooled on the table. "No it's not," he moaned. He pushed himself away from the table and sat staring at Charlie and Mike. "Is Darla Jean alive?"

Mike shook his head.

"You know she's not," Charlie answered soothingly.

Jason threw his hands up and slurred, "Then how can it be all right?"

Mike shoved a hot cup of coffee into Jason's hands. "Drink it. All of it, now."

Jason sipped with his eyes cast to the floor.

"Why did Becky take those pills?" Charlie stood with his arms crossed as he stared at Jason's greasy hair.

He shrugged, not noticing the coffee spilling out of the cup. "Didn't want to live 'cause of what she'd done."

The gurney with Becky's body rumbled down the hallway past the kitchen.

The reality of what was going on sucker-punched Jason. He jumped up and ran after his wife screaming, "BECKY! DON'T LEAVE ME! PLEASE DON'T LEAVE ME!"

♣

"The doctors said it would be tomorrow before we can talk with her," Luke reported. "And they have Jason sedated."

Charlie rubbed the back of his neck thinking, *how much worse can this day get*? He dropped his hands to his hips, then threw them up into the air. "Well, that's it then. Not much we can do about them now."

"Nope." Luke slapped Charlie's back. "Let's go get some lunch."

"Yeah, I don't want to go back to the pharmacy. Let's go to *The Steakhouse.*"

They drove the ten minutes to the restaurant in silence. Each of them gathered his own thoughts, analyzed what he had seen and heard. Once seated and their orders placed, Charlie began to sort out clues with Luke.

"So Becky took the pills because she couldn't live with what she'd done." Charlie drummed his fingers on the thick wooden table. "The reason could be because Darla Jean was pregnant and blackmailing Matt. Or because Becky couldn't live with the fact she had killed her own daughter."

Luke took a yeast roll from the wire basket the waitress had left earlier. Tearing it in half, he smeared a generous amount of butter on each piece. "And we can't find out until tomorrow, which is most definitely out of the question."

"I wanted this case closed today." Charlie followed Luke's lead with the roll. "We're going to assume she killed Darla Jean until we get proof otherwise. Which means after we finish here, we need to track down Ruth Hoffsteader so we can rule her out as a suspect."

The waitress dropped off their salads and a fresh basket of rolls then informed them their steaks would be up shortly.

Luke snorted, "Do you really think we're going to question her without David?"

Charlie shook his head with a smirk. "Enough about that. I don't want to talk about the case right now. I want to enjoy my steak and think about tomorrow. I need happy thoughts at the moment." He doused the salad with honey mustard dressing. "Remind me what all Ma said we had to do, or not come home?"

"Get Da's tux. We only got ours yesterday," Luke mumbled around a mouth full of lettuce. He held up a finger while he chewed, then swallowed. "And verify your booking for the *Rose Cottage*, and pay Father Eli for performing the ceremony. Stop by *Stan's Liquor Shoppe* and make sure they deliver a case of champagne to the house for tonight. Ma said Da forgot about it, and he'd be busy at the fellowship hall all day setting up the bar and helping her decorate. And ..." Luke twisted his mouth thinking. "Oh, ask Theodore to pick up

Marian at the house tomorrow in the Rolls, and he has to wear the black chauffeur tunic."

Charlie held up five fingers. "Only five things? That's it?"

"Yep."

The waitress dropped the hot steak plates on the table. "Can I get you guys anything else?"

"No," they answered in unison and cut into the rare steaks.

Charlie paused. "Let's get everything done Ma wants, then go to Hoffsteader's office; we'll save Father Eli for last."

"Sounds like a plan."

Chapter 28

"An old boot and a horseshoe? What for?" Marian was flabbergasted as she picked through the "must have" wedding box.

Emma laughed, and in an Irish lilt asked, "Aye, ya wanted a good ol' Irish ceremony didn't ya now?"

"Yeah, but what are they for?"

Picking up the horseshoe, she said, "This you carry with you down the aisle for good luck." She gave it to Marian. "And this ...," Emma said picking up the worn boot. "Is for Ma to throw over your head after you walk out of the church. It's for luck, as well."

"And this strange coin? It's from 1822?" Marian gave the small coin to Emma.

She held the coin up and marveled at its history. "This belonged to our great-grandmother. She wore it in her shoe on her wedding day. And so has every woman who is a McClung or has married a McClung." Emma gave the coin back to Marian.

"And the bells?" Marian rang three bells.

"They belonged to great-grandmother, Granny, and Ma. Wedding presents to remind you of your vows and love for each other when you hear them ring. Someone will ring them at the reception. Probably during the toasts."

"Did Aunt Ella ever marry?" Marian replaced the bells in the box next to the old boot.

"Almost," Emma answered with a sad smile. "Sorta like you in a way. According to Ma, she was engaged to a swell fella, but a month before the wedding, he was killed in a freak accident at work. And she never found anyone else that suited her."

Marian inhaled sharply at the sudden memory of the two men standing at her front door at five o'clock in the morning, informing her that Lee was dead. "How awful for Aunt Ella," she murmured, swallowing back the tears.

Nodding, Emma replied, "Yeah, but enough of the sad talk. On a lighter note, to tell you the truth, Aunt Ella is a bit of a hussy." She giggled and corrected herself, "But not in a bad way, she just loves men." Emma sat on the bed Aunt Ella had been using. "This was my bed. Rachel slept in yours. Well, not exactly. Ma bought new mattresses when she found out you were coming."

Marian sat across from her. After hearing Aunt Ella's story, she knew getting married now was the right thing. But Marian wanted it to be done right. "Everything is happening so fast. Not that I'm complaining, but I'm afraid I'll forget something. Something important."

"Let's see," Emma pulled a notepad and pen from the nightstand. "Let's start with what you're wearing first. You've tried on the dress and veil and it fits. And …"

A smug grin stretched across Emma's face as she picked up a white paper bag. "In here we have …" She pulled out a pair of white lace pumps. "Try them on."

Marian slid in her narrow feet and walked around. "They fit perfectly, but how did you know which size to buy?"

"Pff, that was easy. We called Joan. Now we know what size you wear in everything. And I mean down to your panties," Emma fell back on the bed laughing.

Marian shook her head. Good ol' Joan. Sadness crept over her face. "I wish she could be here." Marian plopped on the bed beside Emma.

Emma sat up. "Hey, stop sulking! It's not like you didn't invite her. She has other obligations. She'd be here if she could. You know that."

"I know but—,"

Digging around in the bag, Emma pulled out something else and held it behind her back. "Joan suggested this." She stood. A delicate nightgown as fine as a bee's wing floated in the air.

Marian touched it in awe. She held it to herself and looked at her reflection. Intricate lace coyly hid her most interesting female bits.

"I don't see you wearing that for any length of time once Charlie boy gets a load of it."

Chuckling, Marian turned and asked, "What else do you have in that bag?"

Emma dumped the contents on the bed. "Let's see. Stockings, bra, panties, magic hanky, and a blue garter." She exhaled heavily. "That takes care of what you'll be wearing. Well, except the jewelry and Ma said she'd take care of that." Seeing the anxious look on Marian's face, Emma grasped her hands and pulled her to sit on the bed next to her.

"You don't need to be worrying yourself about anything. We McClungs have been doing weddings since great grandma. We've got it down to a science."

"But I feel so guilty. I'm not doing anything to help."

Emma scoffed. "Have you forgotten? You gave Ma your credit card and said the sky's the limit? No cost too high?" She whistled. "I don't want to be around when you get that bill."

Marian laughed so hard, tears ran from the corners of her eyes.

Chapter 29

There were two cars in Attorney David Hoffsteader's parking lot: a Mercedes sedan and a Honda Accord. Charlie didn't have to think too hard about which car belonged to David.

The secretary's fingers were flying across the keys of the typewriter as they entered. She stopped typing abruptly when Charlie and Luke stood in front of her desk.

Obviously perturbed by their unscheduled appearance, she asked curtly, "May I be of some assistance?"

"We need to speak with Mr. Hoffsteader," Charlie said. He thought he saw her snarl, or maybe her bun was pulled too tight.

She stood. "I will see if he is available. Please take a seat."

They sat and waited.

The secretary returned within five minutes, carrying an arm-load of legal files. "He will see you now. The last door on the right."

Charlie knocked softly on the ornate office door.

"Come in," sighed David Hoffsteader. "Please be seated." He sat straight with both palms resting on his oversized mahogany desk.

He looks like he's about to face a firing squad, Charlie thought.

David started the conversation. "I thought you gave Matthew the all clear?"

"Well, sir, for the moment." Charlie watched David's fingers twitch and his Adam's apple dip with a nervous swallow.

David stood, turning his back toward them as he poured two fingers of scotch, neat. "May I offer you gentlemen a beverage? Scotch or perhaps bourbon?"

They waved away his offer. Charlie looked at Luke with a slight nod.

Clearing his throat, Luke began. "We heard your wife is planning to leave town for an extended amount of time."

"Yes, what of it?" David eyed him as he sipped his drink.

Luke leaned in. "Was this planned or did something come up suddenly? Say since Tuesday night?"

The attorney set the tumbler down slowly and pursed his lips. "Her plans were moved forward a bit due to the stress of past events." He lifted the glass to his lips and added, "Surely, you can understand."

Tapping his lip, Luke tilted his head. "You see, from our viewpoint, it looks a wee bit shady."

A quizzical expression masked David's face. "Shady? Are you suggesting that my wife has something to do with Darla Jean's death?"

Luke shrugged.

He chuckled, "That's absurd." David stood and refilled the tumbler. "What possible motive would Ruth have?" Ambling to the front of his desk, he sat on the corner giving them a casual, nonchalant appearance. But there was sweat beading on his forehead.

"The theory is that both you and your wife knew about Darla Jean's pregnancy. And your wife was none too happy about it. Especially, when you surprised her with wanting to take full custody of it."

David retreated behind his desk. "The '*it*' was our first grandchild."

Charlie smiled and hoped Luke would catch David's mistake.

"So you don't deny you both knew."

Charlie cheered inside. *Bingo! Luke is getting the hang of this.*

"Well, I suppose. Maybe. But I still don't make the connection to why you think Ruth was involved in this unpleasant matter." David covered his mouth with his index fingers.

Luke stood and began to pace around the office. "You see, what I think is she didn't want to be tied down again. Matt was out of the house. That left just the two of you." He looked at David. "Do you see now where this is heading?"

David smirked. "Oh, please, continue. I'm enjoying this farcical tale."

Luke stopped beside the desk. Putting his open hands on the desktop, he leaned his body toward David Hoffsteader. "She knew you had your mind made up. You were going to adopt the child, sticking her with raising it."

Charlie was impressed as Luke began to pace again.

"Ruth didn't want any part of raising this bastard baby. She didn't know for sure it was her grandchild. Matt told you both of Darla Jean's sudden onset of sexual desires. Hell, it could've been Scottie's, Father Eli's, anybody's." Luke leered and pointed at David. "For all Ruth knew, it could have even been yours."

David pulled back as if Luke was threatening to stab him.

Charlie almost jumped up and yelled, *Yeah, Luke, you got him on the run now.*

"Oh, yeah, she thought it was your bastard child and she didn't want any part of it." Luke threw up his hands. "I mean who could blame her?"

David shook his head. "No, you've got it all wrong—."

Luke sliced off the attorney's excuse. "Ruth was tired of both of the men in her life. Kowtowing to your every need and whim. With Matt gone, she was almost free. And then you tell her she's going to raise another child. No discussion. No way! She had to put an end to that."

"NO! That's not it." David started to get up.

Luke glared at the attorney. "Be quiet and sit down." Satisfied his command was obeyed, he continued. "Ruth would have to get rid of her problem, her hindrance to freedom. Darla Jean Rogers! All she had to do was get Darla Jean alone. I mean your wife is more than capable of snapping Darla Jean's twig of a neck."

David jumped up and slammed his fist on his desk. "I've had enough of this, this, this …" his face was almost purple as he searched for the words. "Just get out of my office. Get out!"

Luke looked at Charlie with a smug grin.

"Sir, we need for you to bring your wife to the station for questioning. You may want to bring an attorney with you," Charlie instructed David.

David frowned. "For what reason? Why should I bring an attorney? I can represent my wife."

Charlie tugged his earlobe. "Well, that may be the case. But are you sure she wants you? You two can work out that situation. You'll need one as well. Not unless you think you're capable of representing both of you."

"What? Why do I need one?"

"You're an attorney, figure that out for yourself." Charlie turned to leave. "Oh, we need you both in the station before the end of the day. I'm getting married tomorrow." He walked out with a satisfied grin.

Chapter 30

Marian stood with Emma's elbow hooked in hers, mainly to keep her from falling over. Emma beamed with pride over her family's elegant interior design skills. The fellowship hall had been transformed into a magical fairyland.

"Ma! How could y'all have done this all in one day?"

Emma hopped from foot to foot. "See, I told you not to worry."

"I've got to sit down. I'm overwhelmed." Marian watched the McClung clan and their friends buzzing around the room.

Da pulled out the closest chair. It was sheathed in white linen with a lavender organza chair sash. The table was covered in fine white linen as well. In the center of each round table was a clear cylindrical vase filled with tall gnarled twigs woven with clear fairy lights. Marian guessed there was seating for at least 300 people.

"Come with me, my love," beckoned Ma. "I want to show ya where ya be sittin' with ya new husband."

At the far end of the hall was a long rectangle table and chairs with the same linens and sashes. The only exception were the two chairs in the center resembling padded thrones. The McClung family crest hung front and center on the table.

"Oh, Ma and Da," sighed Marian as she kissed each one. "I don't know what to say. I …" She fanned her face with both hands. "I think I'm going to cry. It's all so unreal."

"Tah, tis nothing, iffin' we had more time this room would be a show- stopper," scoffed Da.

Marian turned in a circle trying to take it all in. "I don't believe it could be more beautiful." She looked up at the draped ceiling, back-lit with lavender fairy lights. "I mean even the ceiling … every inch of the room … it's all so breathtaking."

She embraced her new family, clinging to them as she wept. A tissue appeared before Marian. Laughing, she took it and blotted her face. "Where do these tissues come from?"

"I don't even know the answer to that question," groaned Ma. "It's a closely guarded secret by all McClung males."

Marian could hear pots clanging and people chattering from within the kitchen. Rich aromas tantalized her nose. She started toward the kitchen to investigate.

Ma grabbed her arm. "No. Ya not allowed in there. Ya gotta have some surprises for tomorrow."

"But—,"

"Emma, get her outta here," ordered Da. "Get!"

Marian balked. "Can I go inside the church?"

"That's a brilliant idea. Go find Josephine. You need to discuss the ceremony with her. Emma, help Marian locate Josephine, then come back and help us finish up."

♣

"Wait here in the sanctuary while I track down Josephine." Emma left Marian sitting in the front pew.

Silence cloaked the church as she imagined standing at the altar with Charlie. Tomorrow seemed surreal. Three months ago she never dreamed anyone could take Lee's place in her heart. A twinge of guilt gripped her heart. Marian heard Lee's voice reminding her, *Open a new book.*

The hair on Marian's neck stood at attention. She could feel someone watching her. Standing, she turned slowly, eyes searching for the voyeur. There was no one. But the shadows - someone could be secreted there waiting to ... The urge to run away and hide was overpowering. *Stop being a scaredy cat for Pete's sake. It's a church*, Marian scolded herself. She decided to pray, but before she could close her eyes, Emma returned.

"What's the matter? You're not getting cold feet are you?" Emma sat next to Marian and rubbed her back. "You look like you've seen a ghost."

Marian chuckled nervously, "No, uh, I thought … nothing, it's nothing." She smiled as if she believed what she said. "Did you find Josephine?"

"No, but I found Father Eli. He wants to speak with you."

Marian stood and looked over her shoulder searching the shadows. "Sounds great."

Emma's brow crinkled as she followed Marian's gaze. "Sure you're okay?"

"Yeah, fine. Let's go see Father Eli."

Chapter 31

Charlie and Luke watched their suspects behind the two-way mirror. David and Ruth Hoffsteader sat in silence. The longer they sat, the more agitated Ruth grew. David, on the other hand, studied his manicured fingernails and scribbled on a legal pad.

"What's taking them so long?" snapped Ruth. "And stop doodling." She shoved the pad.

David's Montblanc pen slid across the pad. Replacing the cap, he put it in his pocket, thankful she didn't grab it and sling it across the room. Her temper had become increasingly more violent over the past year. He wondered if it was a woman thing, but was afraid to ask.

"Ruth, darling, please be patient. This is a silly ploy the police use," he said looking directly at the mirror.

She rolled her eyes. "Oh, that's easy for you to say. You're not the one forced to come here. You're not the one they want to question." Ruth glared at her husband. "And exactly what did you say or imply for them to even begin to think I had anything to do with that girl's murder?"

"Please calm down. You're getting worked up over nothing."

In a flash, Ruth turned and gripped her husband's wrist.

Charlie saw panic in David's eyes.

"Calm down! You want me to calm down." Spit flew from her bright red lips. "This is all your fault. You and Matthew. If you both could keep your pants on, maybe I wouldn't get worked up. Have you ever thought about that? Have you ever considered how that might affect me?"

David pried her claws off his wrist and said nothing.

Ruth crossed her arms. "Of course not," she hissed through gritted teeth.

Charlie was puzzled by Ruth's behavior. Just two days ago, she was the meek, supportive wife and mother. Now it would appear she was ready to throw both her husband and son to the wolves. He wondered what had changed. Maybe it was the fact that David was trying to implicate her in Darla Jean's murder.

And why would David do that? To deflect suspicion from himself? Or maybe he loved his son more than his wife if he loved her at all. None of the three really had airtight alibis.

Charlie wondered if they were all guilty in one way or another. From where he stood, the Hoffsteader family had mental problems. Each time he questioned them, they played their parts so well, so convincingly, even though the stories changed. Something just wasn't right in their brains.

Luke broke his contemplations. "That family is screwed up big time. It's dog eat dog in there."

"Yeah, I had the same thought." Charlie took a deep breath, "Well, I say we head on in there. Do you want to take the lead?"

"Hmm, I think I'll let you handle Ruth, but I want David." Luke grinned, "He hates me now. I'd like to pick up where I left off."

"Sounds good. Let's go."

Charlie entered the small room with Luke trailing behind. He smiled as he spoke softly to her. "Hello, Mrs. Hoffsteader. Do you mind if I call you Ruth?"

She sat forward with a sweet expression and extended the delicate hand that had tortured her husband a few moments ago. "Please, I would like that."

Charlie turned on his charm. "May I offer you something to drink?" He asked while he held her hand longer than necessary.

"My throat is a little parched. A Diet Coke would be most refreshing. Thank you for asking, Charlie," Ruth purred.

Gruffly, Luke asked David. "And what about you?"

David sneered, "No, thank you, Officer O'Sullivan."

Smirking, Luke thought *I got him where I want him.* He returned quickly with Ruth's soda.

"Now, let's begin with a simple question, Ruth." Charlie paused and waited for her to take a sip. "As I recall, you didn't see Matt return home from his date, nor can you say for sure where your husband was the night Darla Jean was murdered. Is that correct?" He could almost see her mind turning as she tried to select the least condemning answer.

"You are correct."

Charlie shifted his eyes toward her husband. David wore a deadpan expression. "And where were you?"

Ruth took a long drink of soda before she replied. "In bed." She looked into Charlie's eyes and added, "Alone. We have separate bedrooms."

"So, no one can vouch for your whereabouts that night." Charlie wondered what had gone wrong with the Hoffsteader's marriage. Ruth was a very attractive woman for her age. Hardly any wrinkles and her gray eyes sparkled. She had kept her shape over the years. *Maybe money can buy youth but not true love.*

She simply answered, "No."

"Okay, what did you know about your son's relationship with Darla Jean?" Charlie wanted more than yes and no answers.

Ruth tapped the soda can on the table while she pondered his question. Keeping her eyes on the table, she said, "Not much. They've been friends all of their lives." She tilted her head from side to side. "I suspected they had a sexual relationship. I'm not an idiot." She looked at David. "I notice things when I do their laundry."

"Did he ever mention wanting to marry her or hint at her pregnancy?"

Finishing the Diet Coke, Ruth asked for water. "David had plans for Matthew's future which didn't include a wife or baby. That is until he finished school."

Charlie leaned forward. "I understand. Perhaps you may have overheard your son and husband discussing Darla Jean."

"Well, I—"

"Ruth, do not answer that question," ordered David. He cleared his throat. "Detective McClung, you should know better than to ask Ruth that question."

She started to protest, then decided to obey her husband and clamped her lips tightly.

Luke scoffed, "And why is that Mr. Hoffsteader?"

"It's a very simple answer that even you should know detective. I'm not admitting that there was anything for my wife to overhear, but anything she may claim to have heard is strictly hearsay," David sneered.

Charlie inhaled deeply to control his mounting anger. "Ruth, I'll get to the point. The theory is that David told you that *you* were going to raise that baby. Is that correct?"

Ruth stared at her manicured hands resting on her lap. Her jaws tightened, but no words slipped past her lips.

Determined, Charlie said, "That didn't make you happy. You didn't know if it was your son's baby, or your husband's. Either way, you wanted no part of it. You wanted out. You wanted your own life. That's why you killed Darla Jean."

Ruth chuckled as she raised her head slowly. Her eyes fixed on Charlie. "You have most of it right."

David grabbed his wife's forearm. "Shut up Ruth!" He took a deep breath. "As your attorney, I advise you not to say another word. They have no solid evidence. They're just fishing." He gently cupped her cheek and said, "As your husband, I'm begging you to be careful what you say. I love you, darling."

A faint smile touched Ruth's lips but quickly slipped away. "You're my attorney first." She tilted her head back and laughed. "You almost had me with 'I love you' and 'darling' was a nice touch. But it's always been business first with you. I have a nickname for you, Mr. Dom. David first, others second, and me of course, last."

"Ruth, please—."

"No! No more, please. I'm sick and tired of pleasing you." She looked at Charlie. "Yes, he wanted me to raise that bastard. And no, I didn't want any part of it. And yes—."

David slapped his hand across Ruth's mouth. Through bared teeth, he annunciated each word. "No more from you."

Luke slammed his hands on the table. "You know what? I've had it with both of you. I can't decide if I should feel sorry for your miserable life together, or throw you both in jail." He stood and glared at them like a vulture at road kill. He looked to Charlie for the next move.

Charlie's hands were under the table, visible only to his brother-in-law. He tapped his watch then motioned for Luke to get rid of the pair.

"I advise both of you to go home and think about what your options are." Luke sighed and scratched his head. "We'll uncover the truth. I want both of you back here on Monday with your son. Ruth, maybe you should think about getting your own attorney." He growled, "Now, get out of here."

Charlie and Luke went to the break room after the Hoffsteaders left. They stood staring at the vending machine.

Charlie walked away from the snacks, deciding to save his appetite for whatever Ma had planned for dinner. "Well, that was interesting," replied Charlie. "But … I can't shake the feeling that I'm missing something. That they aren't the ones. AUGH! We're running out of time before Ma wants us home. Let's go talk to Father Eli."

Chapter 32

Emma escorted Marian into Father Eli's office. "Here she is."

"Ah, the blushing bride-to-be." He kissed both of Marian's cheeks and motioned her to sit.

"Father, I've got to get back to the fellowship hall." Emma dashed off without waiting for a response.

Marian laughed. "Well, it looks like just the two of us."

"Yes." Father Eli smiled warmly and sat in the chair next to her. "So, let's chat about the wedding. Questions?"

Her mind went blank. "I've really not had much time to think about it. But I'm guessing it will be a traditional Catholic wedding with the mass first then the vows."

"Yes, it's what Mary Kathleen suggested, but if you would like something different we need to discuss it now. Oh, Mary Kathleen also suggested the traditional Irish vows."

Marian pulled her head back, "Irish vows?"

"Ah, yes, you're not Irish." Father Eli went behind his desk and pulled out a sheet of paper from a file. "Here's a copy. Very simple, but I find them more touching than traditional vows."

Reading the vows, Marian pressed her fingertips to her lips. "They're lovely. Yes, I want these." She held the paper for Father Eli to take.

"No, you keep it, I have tons of copies. There's still a very strong Irish presence in Mercy City. I do at least one Irish wedding a month.

All of the McClung's have married Irish. Come to think of it, you're the first non-Irish in the family."

Now Marian felt truly honored to be part of an all-Irish family.

He returned to sit next to Marian. "Now you understand there will be no rehearsal here at the cathedral before the wedding. The Rogers have arranged a community-wide Rosary to be said tonight. Even though Becky is in the hospital. I understand Jason will be able to attend."

"Oh, no," gasped Marian, "What happened?"

Father Eli shook his head, "It's so sad. Becky was overcome with grief and well ... she wanted to be with her daughter."

Suicide. Marian shivered, remembering Diane. "I didn't know. I'll light a candle for her."

"She'll be okay physically, but she'll need a lot of prayers to see her through this awful ordeal," Father Eli mumbled the last few words.

Marian could see he was on the verge of tears. "Emma looked for Josephine earlier but couldn't find her. Is she here?"

He swallowed his grief. "Yes, let me ring her."

"There's no need, Eli." Josephine entered the room silently. With a hard quizzical look, she asked Marian, "Do you want something ..." she paused. Smiling sweetly, she asked again. "What may I do for you?"

She was going to say "something else." Does she think I'm being demanding? Marian wondered.

Father Eli frowned then coughed. "Josephine, we were discussing the wedding."

Josephine stood stone-faced.

Marian stood and clasped Josephine's cold boney hand. "I was wondering if you would be able to walk me through the ceremony."

Her eyes questioned her brother. "What, no rehearsal tonight?"

"Remember, the Rosary for Darla Jean tonight?"

Shaking her head as if she had just awakened from a dream, Josephine, replied, "Oh, yes, I'm sorry. I don't know where my mind is today." She patted Marian's hand. "I will be more than happy; come follow me. Afterward, we'll have some tea. How does that sound?"

Marian wondered if Josephine was having a bad day and decided to be extra considerate. *We all battle demons at one time or another.* "Oh, that sounds divine. How kind of you, Josephine."

She and Josephine bumped into Charlie and Luke as they left Father Eli's office.

"Marian!" Charlie hugged her and planted a healthy kiss on her lips. "The best part of my day." He looked at Josephine and wondered why she always looked so depressed. "Where are you two going?"

"Josephine is being a dear and walking me through the ceremony. Isn't she sweet?"

Charlie knew Marian well enough that she was being extra gushy for a reason. He wondered what had happened in Father Eli's office. But he looked at Josephine's menacing face and decided that he wouldn't want her for an enemy. *Hmm, that's strange she's not wearing earrings. Josephine always wears her mother's pearl earrings.* Then he remembered she was missing one the last time they spoke.

"I see you haven't found the missing earring." Charlie pointed to Josephine's naked earlobes. "Don't worry, it'll turn up sooner or later."

Josephine blushed. "Oh, I'd forgotten about it. I've had so much on my mind lately."

Charlie gave Marian a peck on her cheek. "I don't want to keep you. Besides, we need to speak to Father Eli. I'll see you tonight."

♣

"Knock, knock." Charlie poked his head into Father Eli's office. "May we come in?"

Father Eli greeted them with a warm handshake and a sad smile. "I just had a pleasant visit with your Marian. Such a delight. You are a very lucky man."

"I wake up every morning and thank God she's real, not a dream." Charlie pulled out his wallet. Handing Father Eli five, folded one hundred dollar bills, he said, "This can't even begin to express my appreciation."

Father Eli took them and immediately put them in the center desk drawer. "It's entirely my pleasure to see the day your granny prayed for." He motioned for them to sit as he sat on the front edge of his desk. "It doesn't take both of you to tip me for performing the ceremony, so I'm going to take an educated guess that you're here to discuss Darla Jean's murder again."

"I hate to agree with you, Father but our list of suspects is getting shorter. And I don't like telling you this, but you're still on it," Charlie sighed.

Father Eli smiled sadly. "Well, I can understand that. What can I say to change your minds?'

"Father, can you give us a solid alibi?" pleaded Luke.

"No son, that I cannot do."

Charlie scratched his neck. "We heard you and Josephine had quite an argument this morning. Can you explain that?"

Father Eli heaved a sigh and shut his office door. "I don't want anyone overhearing this conversation."

Charlie's eyebrows shot up with curiosity.

Father Eli plopped behind his desk. Leaning back, he stared at the ornate ceiling, musing where to start. "Something is wrong with Josephine. More than her usual moodiness."

"Can you elaborate?" Charlie could see the concern on his face.

He shrugged. "It's hard to put a finger on it. It's like … like she hates me. Hates being here."

Charlie drummed his fingers on the arm of the chair. "Hmm, when did this start? Recently?"

Father Eli blinked as he thought. "I guess around three months ago."

Luke leaned forward. "That's around the time Darla Jean returned from the aspirancy program at the convent. Did something happen between the two of them?"

"To be honest with you, I don't know. But it appeared to me their relationship was different. Strained maybe, sort of a love-hate feeling between the two?" Father Eli tossed up his hands. "I don't know. Women? Who can figure them out?"

Charlie was intrigued. "The argument this morning must've been a heated one for it to be in the rumor mill already."

"Yep, that it was." Father Eli sighed heavily. "I think the stress of the past few days has finally gotten the best of her. But I'm not sure what made her snap." He walked around the desk and leaned back against the front. "Josephine followed me into the office after morning mass, her voice getting louder and more venomous with each word that spewed from her mouth."

Father Eli rubbed the back of his neck. "Just thinking about it makes me ... shudder." He contemplated their conversation. "Please remember, Josephine has dedicated her life to the church, to me. She's a caring soul. But she has a certain set of ... standards, rules I guess."

"She must have found out about Darla Jean's newly found *freedom* so to speak. Maybe that's why their relationship soured," Charlie surmised.

Father Eli nodded. "Maybe, it seems she confided in Josephine more than I knew. It would make sense based on some of the things she was ranting about."

"Like what?" Charlie and Luke both asked.

"She said, 'I warned you not to get so chummy with that girl. Now, look what's happened. Rumors are flying around that you killed her because you got her pregnant! I worked too hard for this to happen. For you to throw it all away because of some schoolboy infatuation over a trollop."

Father Eli covered his face with both hands. They slid down, exposing a tormented man. "Josephine said that between me and our papa, we had ruined her. She said she had wanted to be a wife and mother."

He bit the inside of his mouth, his eyes full of tears. "And all she got was the misfortune of raising her brother." Father Eli's mouth twisted. "Then Josephine said that I took away her chance of happiness. That I made her into a non-person, just a beast of burden."

Charlie saw a pitcher of water sitting on the credenza. He poured a glass, handing it to Father Eli. "I'm sorry."

Father Eli finished the water. "Oh, I'm not finished." He began to pace. "She said she felt like an ass for being so naïve thinking her service to me and to God would be fulfilling. As if that was all she needed to make her life complete. Then Josephine started walking around the office, seething like a mad woman. She said something like, everyone around her is falling in love, getting married, and having babies. That she should be happy for their good fortune. But it's not enough to live through others. All she saw were lost opportunities and a wasted life because of me."

Exhausted from reliving the disturbing memory, he sat down and continued. "She stood in front of the window," Father Eli pointed to the one, "and ran her hand down the curtain. Her fingers ran around the tieback. She seemed to calm down. In a flash, she was in my face telling me that I better not disappoint her and make her regret her choices."

"Or what?" Charlie shrugged.

Father Eli shuddered. "I don't know. At the moment, I was terrified of her, so I told her I'd never disappoint her. She appeared to be satisfied and left."

Charlie and Luke sat in silence as they digested Father Eli's replay of the argument.

The tieback. The dream. It made sense now. It was a pearl earring. Charlie jumped up. "We need to find Marian."

Chapter 33

Marian walked slowly around Josephine's sitting room. The antiques decorating the small dark sitting room were stunning. Heavy curtains covered the wide windows. Wondering why Josephine didn't open them to brighten the room, she decided the sunlight would probably make the room too hot. Or maybe Josephine found the dimness soothing.

She was entranced by the pictures of Father Eli, beginning with his birth and progressing to the present. Josephine wore a sad smile in the photos of her alone. But in the ones she shared with her brother, her face seemed to radiate with pride. *Poor Josephine only finds happiness through Father Eli. I wonder if she thinks of him as her son.*

"He's a handsome man," Josephine stated bluntly. "I'm afraid it may be more of a curse than a blessing."

Marian was startled by Josephine's silent appearance and brusque tone. "Oh, um," her hand slapped against her runaway heart. "You mean because of—."

"Yes," she answered, cutting off Marian's question. Josephine set the silver tea service on the coffee table with great care. "The fellowship hall is buzzing. Your new family must love you very much," she said without feeling.

Marian took the steaming cup of tea offered. "Thank you, Josephine. You are so kind. And yes, I agree. I do feel a lot of love from the McClung family."

"Scone? I ran into one of Charlie's sister's in the kitchen. She told me you're partial to them."

"Yes, please." Marian recognized Ma's signature pastry. "Josephine, I really do appreciate you walking me through the proper steps of an Irish wedding. I know you must be terribly busy with such a large congregation. Thank you for your time."

Staring at Marian over the rim of her cup, Josephine wondered if she realized how lucky she was to be marrying Charlie. "It's part of my job. No need to thank me." She topped off Marian's cup.

"But surely sharing tea and scones with me isn't part of your job. And for this I thank you."

Josephine bowed her head slightly, accepting Marian's appreciation.

Looking around the room trying to think of something to fill the uncomfortable silence, Marian said, "I bet after a day's work, just walking into this cozy room relieves your stress. It's so relaxing."

"I suppose, but my work seems unending. Not much time to relax and do nothing. I usually head straight to bed."

Man, what does it take to make this woman smile? Marian decided to take a different route. "So how long have you lived in Mercy City?"

"Eli and I moved here five years ago. He was the youngest priest to take over this parish, only twenty-eight at the time." Josephine's pride shone on her face.

Reaching for a scone, Marian noticed a single pearl earring beside the serving tray. She glanced toward Josephine's earlobes. One of them was a bright pink. "These taste like Ma's recipe."

"Mary Kathleen, or *Ma* as you refer to her, made them for the decorating crew."

After hearing her bitter tone concerning the scones, Marian decided to give up on Josephine. "Well, I think I've overstayed my welcome. Besides, I would like to light a candle for the Rogers and Lee before I head over to the fellowship hall."

"How fortunate you are to have had two loves in your life," Josephine replied with a sour tone and frown.

"Yes, I do feel blessed for having two wonderful men in my life," Marian agreed.

Josephine stood like a live statue and motioned Marian to follow. "I'll show you the prayer closet. It's more private. The sanctuary is too active at this time of day."

Josephine led Marian down an unfamiliar hallway. Their footsteps echoed off the stone walls. "Here it is."

Entering the small room, Marian felt alone and isolated from the outside world. "You're right. It's much more private. Thank you, Josephine."

"Do you think you'll be able to find your way back?"

"Yes, thank you."

Josephine nodded and disappeared down the hallway.

Marian stood inside the poorly lit room, letting her eyes adjust. There wasn't much light cast from the hallway to the inside of the small room. *No windows. Only one way out.* Goosebumps danced up her arms. *For Pete's sake, Marian, it's only a prayer closet,* she reminded herself. *Yeah, but Darla Jean was probably killed somewhere inside this church. Maybe here.* "Stop it!" she scolded herself. "I'll light the candles, pray, then find my way to the fellowship hall. Stop being a fraidy-cat."

She lit two white candles for Lee and Darla Jean, then lit two red ones for the Rogers and for tomorrow. Finding the coin box, she pulled a ten from her wallet and shoved it in the slot. There was an open Bible sitting on a side table with a set of rosary beads lying beside it. Marian carried it to the floor lamp and read a highlighted passage.

Romans 13:4 - For he is the minister of God to thee for good. But if thou do that which is evil, be afraid; for he beareth not the sword in vain: for he is the minister of God, a revenger to execute wrath upon him that doeth evil.

Well, that's not very comforting, she thought and returned it to the table. It had been a long time since she had said a rosary. So she carried it with her to the kneeler. After the rosary, she began to pray, fixing her eyes on the crucifix.

Her eyes traced the lines of the cross. When her eyes trailed to the bottom, a tiny glimmer caught her eye. She squinted to see what was lying on the floor.

Her curiosity was surpassed by the ache in her shins and forearms caused from being pressed against the semi-exposed wood poking through the worn padding. Marian stood and rubbed the pain in her limbs. She could see faint red indentations on her skin.

The glimmer on the floor caught her eye again. Squatting, she reached in between the kneeler and the crucifix. Her fingers felt something cold.

Chapter 34

Charlie ran into the sanctuary with Luke right behind him. The cavernous church was void of life. He ran to the far corners. As Charlie searched the deep dark shadows, all he could think about was the dream. The skeletal hand dragging Marian into the dark abyss. *Oh, God, please not again*, he prayed as his heart pounded. "We've got to find her, Luke. We have to!"

"Calm, down. I'm sure she's okay." Luke clutched his brother-in-law's shoulders and saw sheer terror in his wild eyes. "She and Josephine are probably in the fellowship hall helping with the decorations."

Charlie caught his breath and ran his hand over his forehead. "Yeah, you're probably right."

"Let's get over there before you stroke out on me."

They entered the noisy hall. Charlie's gaze flew around the room searching for Marian. He saw none of the hall's beauty. "She's not here!" Scanning the room one more time, he found Ma. "Ma! Have you seen Marian?"

"She was here a few minutes ago. She's gone to see Father Eli." She frowned, "What's the matter, son?"

"No, she's not there. I just left him and she's not in the church either. Have you seen Josephine?" Charlie asked hurriedly.

"Tah, I forgot. Josephine went to the kitchen to fetch tea and scones for our Marian. She must be in Josephine's sittin' room."

He kissed Ma. "Thanks! If you see her, tell her to stay here with you." Charlie stopped by the kitchen to make sure Marian wasn't sneaking scones. "Damn, not here! Luke, we've got to find her."

He dashed through the vacant sanctuary toward Josephine's rooms. They stopped by Father Eli's office. It was empty. When they entered Josephine's suite, Charlie found evidence of tea and scones. He cupped his hand around the teapot. It was cold and empty and there were plenty of crumbs on the plates. "So Marian was here. But where could she be now?"

Charlie stared at the cup with lipstick, Marian's color. "What's this?" He held up a pearl earring. The round white gem was like a speck of light in the dim sitting room. *The dream.* Dread scratched at the back of his neck, causing his hair to bristle. Charlie returned the earring to where he had found it.

"Something's wrong. We've got to find Marian. Think! Where could she be?" Charlie stepped out into the hallway to escape the prison-like room.

Luke broke his thought. "She wouldn't have left the building without telling someone. So she's got to be here. Maybe Josephine took her on a tour?"

Charlie snapped his fingers. "That's it! The prayer closet! Do you remember how to get there?

Looking up and down the hallway, Luke pointed to the left, "That way to the end and left again."

Charlie jogged to the prayer closet, praying for Marian to be there and be alive.

Chapter 35

Marian strained to grab the tiny object her fingers had touched. "Almost got it, just a little bit more." Grimacing, she stretched as far as she could, pressed her hand down to capture the object, and slid it back toward her.

"Well, what do we have here?" In the dim light, it appeared to be part of a chain. She walked to the floor lamp and held it under the light. After studying it for a few seconds, it dawned on her it was two earrings hooked together.

Carefully, she untangled the jewelry. "Hmm, a gold loop." She giggled. "That's weird. Charlie warned me not to wear gold loops." Marian wondered why. Holding the other earring under the light, she saw it was a single pearl.

"Uh, this looks like the one on Josephine's coffee table." Holding the two together, she began to form scenarios on how the earrings found their way onto the floor and became entwined. Nothing seemed plausible.

Marian considered *if this one is the mate to the one on the coffee table, then Josephine must have lost it in here.* She looked at it more closely. *Yep, definitely a match.* Then she remembered Josephine's bright pink earlobe. *I wondered if it was ripped from her ear. But how could she not feel an earring being torn from her ear?*

Next, she studied the loop. *How did these two get tangled together?*

Marian held them together. "Gold loop. Why was Charlie so concerned about gold loops?"

A memory slammed forward with full force. "I remember!"

Marian's mind began to spin. *That night. They were in the kitchen. I interrupted them. Dylan said something about an earring. They were talking about Darla Jean.*

A hot flash overwhelmed her as she realized that Darla Jean was wearing the earring when she was killed. Which meant she was killed in this room. Marian shoved the earrings into her pants pocket, then snatched up a prayer candle. Holding the candle close to the kneeler, she could see deep scratches in the padding. *But this thing is old. They may mean nothing.*

She replaced the candle and rubbed her aching forearms. Her hand froze on her arm. *I remember seeing bruises on Darla Jean's arms. I wonder...*

Marian knelt on the kneeler, pretending to be Darla Jean. She was bigger than her, but still, she thought it may give her a clue.

Her breath caught as the room darkened. Marian looked toward the door. A looming shadow filled the space. It swayed as if it couldn't decide to come in or leave the occupied room.

Marian froze. Her mouth opened to tell the person she was leaving and they could have the room. But the shadow descended upon her and the words were stifled by the hands around her neck.

Chapter 36

"Did you see that?" Charlie thought he saw someone running around the corner toward the prayer closet.

Luke panted, "Yeah, who was it?"

Charlie picked up his speed. As he rounded the corner, he saw just the heel of someone's foot enter the prayer closet. He could hear muted voices, but couldn't make out who they belonged to. They sounded angry, panicked, and desperate. The sounds of things being knocked around as if a fight or struggle was happening in the room.

Oh, God, not again. This can't be happening, again. "MARIAN!" Charlie yelled as he raced into the dark room. All he could see were glimpses of a blurred blob bouncing off the walls. Lit candles rolled around the floor. The floor lamp had been knocked over, casting bizarre shadows on the ceiling.

Charlie lunged for the shapeless mass. There were too many arms to be just one person. Too many to be two. "MARIAN, ARE YOU IN HERE? ANSWER ME DAMMIT!" he commanded as Luke helped him untangle the angry human mass.

Hearing a shriek of terror, Charlie realized it was Marian. He yanked one creature off, tossing it like a rag doll toward the door. It thwacked against the floor and cried out in pain. Two were left. Luke held on to the taller of the two. Charlie gave it a right hook then an upper jab. It released its prey with a banshee howl.

Luke dragged the limp being out of the prayer closet while Charlie attended to the one gasping for air and coughing.

"Marian?" Charlie knew it was her as soon as he wrapped his arms around her. Burying his face in her hair, his tears took control.

He picked her up. As he stepped into the hallway, Charlie saw Father Eli with a trickle of blood on his forehead and a frazzled Luke attending Josephine. She was unconscious, sporting the badges on her face from Charlie's punches. He wanted to give her a swift kick, instead, he kissed Marian.

He chuckled, "Why do women want to kill you?"

Marian started to speak.

"No, don't say a word until the paramedics arrive."

She obeyed. Pressing her face against his shoulder, she sobbed.

"You've every right to cry. Hell, I even cried back there. You're safe now." Charlie kissed her temple. "But sweetheart, you've got to stop doing this." He felt her tremble as she attempted to laugh.

♣

Mary Grace told the paramedic, "You guys can go. I can handle it from here." She gave Marian another cup of water. "Drink slowly." Mary Grace looked at her Uncle Charlie. "I'll stay with her tonight just in case she needs me." She turned her attention back to Marian. "I'm warning you, Marian, we'll be on you like ugly on an ape if you don't obey our orders. Won't we, Joan?"

"Yep, she knows not to cross me." Joan leaned over from the chair next to her best friend and grabbed her hand. "Charlie, handcuff us together. That should do the trick."

Marian nodded and tried not to laugh.

Charlie peeled Ma's arms from around his waist. "Thanks you two." He hugged his niece and then kissed Marian on the forehead. Nose to nose, he instructed Marian, "And you be a good patient, understand or …?" He shook his handcuffs at her.

Marian kissed his nose and gave him a salute.

"Joan, I'm trusting you and Mary Grace to protect my Marian. Understand?"

Rolling her eyes at Charlie, Joan replied, "Aye-aye captain."

Marian hugged Joan and murmured in her ear, "I'm so happy you're here."

"Me, too." Joan looked at Ma. "I was the reason Ma warned you away from the kitchen. Surprise!" She tapped Marian's lips with her finger. "And no talking or whispering. I mean no sound from these today," scolded Joan. "You'll be wanting to save that voice for tomorrow's celebration." Joan leaned so close to Marian her lips touched her ear. Joan's next words were meant for Marian's ears only. "And moaning for the honeymoon. You know what I mean."

Marian blushed then gasped. *The wedding*. Her gaze ran around the crowded room. She held one of Charlie's magical tissues. Pressing it to the corners of her eyes, she mouthed the words, "Wedding? What about the wedding?"

"We can't be havin' no weddin'." Da shook his head. "No, not afta this."

Marian clasped her hands prayerfully and begged silently, "Please. Please."

"You can't be serious, Mr. McClung?" whined Joan.

Aunt Ella spoke, "Sure, we'll be havin' the weddin'." She put her hands on her hips and dared her brother otherwise. "John Patrick McClung, I won't be havin' none of ya lip. Everything is done. We're set to go. And Joan didn't come all this way just to see us. Mary Grace, my pet, our Marian will be right as rain by mornin'?"

Mary Grace shrugged, "Her voice more than likely will be back to normal so yeah, right as rain."

"I'll be givin' ya that, but what about a priest. Ya not be marryin' without no priest," countered Da.

From the far back corner of his office, Father Eli spoke up. "I'll be your priest, that is if you still want me." He came forward and knelt before Marian. "Can you ever forgive me?"

Marian held his face between her hands. Kissing his forehead, she croaked, "You've done nothing wrong, Father. You tried to save me."

Charlie pulled him away from Marian and into a bear hug. "Father, if not for you, she..." He closed his eyes forcing away the bitter alternative. "Thank you."

Chapter 37

Mike Purvis sat outside Josephine's hospital room thinking, *this only happens in the movies*. He stood when he saw Charlie and Luke striding toward him with a nurse and Dr. Leech. He was surprised by Charlie's calm demeanor as he shook his friend's hand.

"Has she said anything?" asked Charlie.

Mike sighed, "Not a peep."

"Hmm, alright let's go in."

Luke held back Charlie. "Are you sure you can do this? I mean, she just tried to kill the love of your life. Honestly, are you ready to confront her?"

Nodding, Charlie replied, "I've got to know why."

The four of them entered the room. Josephine's bruised eyes were closed, her breathing regular. Her wrists were handcuffed to the railings.

Charlie gently held her hand and whispered, "Josephine, are you awake?"

She cracked her puffy eyes. "Where's Eli? Is he alright?" Her swollen lips barely moved.

"He's fine. He's at the church."

"That's right. The rosary's tonight." Josephine's hand was stayed by the loose handcuff. A look of confusion clouded her face.

Charlie would have felt pity for her if she hadn't tried to strangle Marian. "Why did you try to kill Marian?"

Tears escaped from her closed eyes, but Josephine was silent.

"Why did you kill Darla Jean Rogers?"

She answered with closed eyes. "What other choice did I have? She was bad, so very wicked."

"I don't understand, Josephine, please explain it to me," Charlie cajoled. "Why didn't you have a choice?"

She sighed. "Can I have some water?"

Charlie held the straw to her lips as she drank.

Josephine turned her head and gazed at Charlie. "Thank you. You're a good man." Looking away, she stared out the window. "Darla Jean was going to ruin everything. But I don't know why she wanted to. From the outside, Darla Jean was a good girl, but her core was rotten." She looked at Charlie. "You know what I'm saying?"

"I think so, but tell me how you knew she was."

"Darla Jean was in love with worldly pleasures. She told me she was pregnant and implied it could be anyone's child." Josephine nodded. "She meant Eli. I didn't believe it. But when he gave her his rosary beads just because she asked for it." Tears gathered as her mouth twisted. "It belonged to our mother. And then he sold our grandmother's armoire for her. What was I supposed to think? What?"

Charlie held her hand as she cried and wiped her face dry. "Come on, Josephine, finish telling me why."

Josephine said through clenched teeth, "I devoted my life to Eli. I had no life. And that's how he repays me. I gave up everything. Then he starts taking away my treasured mementos for her!"

Her face hardened. "Then that night. That night, she came into my room. I had just closed the curtains. I was tired and wanted to go to bed. But Darla Jean just had to give me some good news. She tells me Matthew's going to give her one hundred thousand dollars to take care of his child. And wouldn't that make the sisters at the convent happy? Then she skips off to the prayer closet."

"Charlie, may I have some more water?" After she drank, Josephine continued. "Then Eli stops by and tells me to check on Darla Jean. He didn't even say goodnight to me. So I went after her. There she was praying and acting all surprised to see me. Really? Darla Jean tells me that all along she knew it was Matthew's baby. So I asked her why she led Eli to believe it was his baby. She said how could it be Eli's baby when he never even touched her. He didn't even know she was pregnant. Darla Jean said that my mind was warped to think such an awful thing about my own brother."

Her lips trembled. "Darla Jean had the nerve to laugh at me when I asked about the rosary and armoire. She said I shouldn't be surprised by that." In a mimicking voice, Josephine said, "Isn't it obvious? He loves me more than you. I mean look at me. Who could refuse such a pretty and desirable young thing like me?"

Josephine blinked as she was trying to find the courage to continue. "She said … she said, just look at yourself, who in God's world could ever love a pathetic, old, ugly cow like you. You're like Quasimodo hiding in the church."

She paused, her chest heaving. Her eyes staring at the memory only she could see. "All I could think was I was the good girl. Not her, yet she was the one blessed with beauty and charm. Everything! And then … and then she rubs my nose in it by comparing me to Quasimodo."

Josephine looked at her hands held by the handcuffs. "I was still holding the tieback. And I just …" Josephine's head fell back on the pillow and wailed.

Charlie waited for her to calm down. "But why Marian? What did she say to you to make you want to kill her?"

Josephine violently tossed her head. "Nothing, nothing at all," she sobbed. "I was so upset knowing …"

Confused, Charlie squeezed her hand. "Josephine, please tell me why you wanted Marian dead? Please."

Josephine inhaled deeply and held the breath. Slowly, she released it and gave him a pitiful smile. She looked at each person in the room, seeing their stunned expressions. "You'll think me mad," she said to Charlie.

"Go on, tell me why."

She smiled again, "I'm so sorry, Charlie, can you ever forgive me? Can you?"

He nodded.

"Thank you." She closed her eyes not wanting to witness his reaction. "I was in love with you once." Josephine felt his hand twitch on hers. "I know, but you're a very handsome man and I'm a silly old fool."

With a grunt, she admitted, "I've had many infatuations over these long, lonely years. But not one of them … not a single …" Josephine strangled a sob and whispered, "All I wanted was someone to love me, to hold me, to want me. Just one time that's all, even if it was just for one moment." She squeezed her eyes tightly and tossed her head from side to side. She bared her teeth as if she were trying to keep a demon from escaping. After a few moments, she lay in still silence.

Josephine looked out the window. "Marian is very beautiful. No one's ever said that about me. I'm just an unlovable, ugly, old cow."

She looked at Charlie with tear-filled eyes. "When Marian told me that she has had two great loves in her life … I just … snapped."

Chapter 38

Uilleann bagpipers played *Haste to the Wedding*, as Charlie and Marian exited the church in a hail of birdseed. Out of the corner of her eye, Marian saw Ma with the old boot. She poked Charlie in the ribs with her elbow and nodded her head toward Ma.

Charlie yelled, "Watch out for the boot!"

The wedding party roared with laughter as the boot sailed over Marian's head. They stood on the bottom stone step of the cathedral while cameras flashed.

Marian felt like a fairytale princess as they entered the magnificently decorated fellowship hall and then sat on the throne-like chair. After yesterday's events, she felt truly blessed. Her hand touched the wide multi-strand choker covering the bruises on her neck. She laughed at the irony of it as Ma fastened it around her neck.

Dinner was served while Sophia played the harp and her brother, Ryan, played the violin. When the meal began to wind down, the champagne and mead began to flow freely with the sound of the pipers.

Da stood and rang one of the three bells. "Ah, it's time for me to be toasting me new daughter, Marian, and me son." He lifted his glass. "May there always be work for ya hands to do. May ya purse always hold a coin or two. May the sun always shine on ya window pane. May a rainbow be certain to follow each rain. May the hand of a friend always be near ya. May God fill ya heart with gladness to cheer ya!"

The room reverberated with the shout of, "Slainte!"

Mike Purvis cleared his throat and rang the second bell. "May God bless your home with the peace that surpasses understanding. May your troubles be less and your blessings be more. And nothing but happiness come in your door. Long live the Irish. Long live their cheer. Long live our friendship year after year."

"Slainte!"

Joan rang the third bell. "May your hands be forever clasped in friendship and your hearts joined forever in love."

"Slainte!"

Charlie stood. "Marian, shall we dance?"

Marian fastened her eyes on her new husband's face as they danced. The cheer from the guests seemed distant. "I want to say our vows again."

Charlie rested his forehead against hers. Together they pledged, "By the power that Christ brought from heaven, mayst thou love me. As the sun follows its course, mayst thou follow me. As light to the eye, as bread to the hungry, as joy to the heart, may thy presence be with me, oh one that I love, 'til death comes to part us asunder." Time seemed to stand still as they kissed.

Da bumped into Charlie, breaking the spell. "Aye, son, be saving that for tonight." He winked at them. "Now make some room. Ya Ma and me will be dancing a jig. Take our hands."

He looked around for his clan. Giving one high pitched whistle, his family joined them. They formed a circle, clasping hands. Da yelled, "It's time boys." The sound of a banjo, fiddle, guitar, and flute filled the room. The McClung clan began to dance. Eventually, all the guests joined in.

After 30 minutes the music stopped, the dancers happy for a bit of rest. Sophia and Ryan resumed playing the harp and violin. Aunt Ella, wearing an ivory bonnet with a wide purple band and oversized flower, took over the show. She and Joan pushed a large round table to the middle of the dance floor. In the center of the table was the wedding cake. Aunt Ella's creation was her gift to her nephew and his new wife.

The cake consisted of four enormous graduating layers covered with off-white fondant with a ribbon of the same fondant cascading from the top layer and puddling around the bottom. Clutches of lavender were the only other decoration. Each layer was a different flavor, chocolate, hummingbird, and lemon. The top layer was Marian's favorite, cream cheese pound cake. The layers were separated with cream cheese buttercream.

Together, Marian and Charlie held the pearl-handled knife and cut the first piece. Charlie licked the hummingbird cake crumbs from the knife then offered it to Marian who licked as well. She whispered in Charlie's ear. "I'm ready for the honeymoon."

He grinned. "We'll toss the garter and bouquet and then be on our way."

Da and Sean carried Marian's chair to the center of the floor. She sat down while Charlie knelt before her. He slowly pushed up her gown as far as modesty allowed, exposing a pearl-studded blue garter.

The guests cheered and whistled while Charlie removed it with his teeth.

All the single men lined up, hoping to catch the dainty garter. James, Charlie's youngest nephew caught it. Next, all the single women bunched together in anticipation of catching the bouquet. Marian turned her back and flipped the bouquet behind. She turned in time to see Joan catch it.

James strolled over to Joan. "Well, it looks like we'll be getting married."

Joan grinned. "How old are you?"

Stretching to full height, he said in his most manly voice, "I'm fourteen about to turn fifteen."

"Mmm, marry them young and raise them the way you want them. That's what my Mama preached." Joan, not much taller than James, pulled him into a playful hug.

James laughed, "We'll set a date." He turned and looked at his mother, Emma, and asked, "When can I get married?"

The guests roared with laughter.

♣

The Rolls Royce pulled up to the brightly lit bed and breakfast. The porch railings were wrapped in white organza with lavender and roses tucked in here and there. Theodore jumped out and opened the door. Charlie swooped Marian into his arms and carried her into the house and into their suite.

Theodore dropped their luggage just inside the room. He tipped his hat and shut the door.

Soft music was playing. A table for two held chocolate-covered strawberries, chilled shrimp, and a platter of cheeses, grapes, and crackers. A silver champagne bucket held a bottle of Dom Perignon. Charlie kissed her passionately.

Breathlessly she asked, "So are we going to eat first or …?"

Charlie shook his head with a leering grin as he tossed his jacket onto a nearby chair and unbuttoned his shirt.

"Hold on big boy. Let me slip into something more … suitable." She snatched her small case and fled into the bathroom.

When she reappeared, the overhead light was turned off. The room was bathed in the warm flickering light of a dozen or so candles strategically placed around the room. Charlie was sitting cross-legged in the chair where his jacket had landed. All he was wearing was a pleased grin and holding two flutes of champagne.

Marian watched Charlie's eyes trail from her face down to her feet and back up, again. His eyes lingered on the places hidden by the lace.

"I think the champagne can wait," he said as he stood.

Marian's eyes slid down his physique. "Well, from the looks of things, I would say we are both very pleased."

As Emma predicted, the gown was on the floor and they were in the bed in a slow, seductive blink of an eye.

—THE END—

About The Author

I am the author of The Charlie McClung mysteries, including *Brilliant Disguise*. I live in Georgia with my husband of 33 years and counting.

Thank you for taking the time to read *A Good Girl*. If you enjoyed it, please consider telling your friends and posting a short review on Amazon and Goodreads. Word of mouth is an author's best friend and is much appreciated.

You can find me on Facebook, Pinterest, LinkedIn, Goodreads, Google+, and Twitter. Please consider being a member of my Street Team. Charlie and Marian look forward to seeing you again as they journey together through mystery, murder, and love.

www.MaryAnneEdwards.com